THE CABIN

JOHN KOLOEN

WATCHFIRE
PRESS

Published by Watchfire Press.

Watchfire Press

www.watchfirepress.com

www.watchfirepress.com/jk

Cover design by Kit Foster

www.kitfosterdesign.com

The Cabin/John Koloen – 1st ed.

ALSO BY JOHN KOLOEN

Insects

Insects: The Hunted

Insects: Specimen

Insects: Books 1, 2 & 3

Griswold's Op

The Cabin

For a complete list of titles, please visit watchfirepress.com/jk.

Visit watchfirepress.com/jk to subscribe to John Koloen's free author newsletter and receive exclusive news and discounts on all of John's upcoming novels.

1

It wasn't that Jacob Alexander was hiding, living as he did on a thickly forested ridge overlooking a tributary of the Flambeau River. He hadn't gone there to escape, he told himself, but to start over, and that required leaving his past behind. He'd been fortunate in that he had enough money to pay for his land in cash and build a cabin overlooking a part of the tributary that beavers had turned into a large pond, its length dependent on rain and snowfall, its width contained by embankments that dropped off into the murky green water.

Across the pond were four small, nearly identical cabins spaced along its length, close enough to the bank to allow fishing from their cramped porches. The edge of the pond was soft with a drop-off that, if you weren't careful, would leave you in the drink, ankle deep in muck. It had happened to him, once. But that's the way it always was. The first time he did anything it seemed he did it wrong. Overlooked the obvious. But he was a quick study, seldom repeating his mistakes.

Married at thirty-five to a twenty-five-year-old whom

he'd mistaken for his soul mate and who'd mistaken him for a bank account. His family had warned him about her. The age difference. For chrissakes, his sister told him, she was in grade school when he graduated from college. She was flighty. Capricious. By comparison, he was a rock, a saver, a planner. An old man before his time. Delaying gratification was something he did without thinking, while she was all about the moment and squeezing it for whatever she could get out of it. Why couldn't his family just stay out of it? he wondered. Why couldn't they just let him be happy? Just this once.

Which was why the marriage was held in the cluttered office of a justice of the peace with two employees as witnesses. Once they were hitched, he thought, his family would come around. They'd see in her what he saw—the joyfulness, the energy, not to mention that she looked fabulous. Men craned their necks when she walked into a room. He saw it everywhere. In restaurants. At the malls. And especially when they were out drinking. She liked to go out. Liked to shop. Liked to dress up. Liked to flash a pouty smile that every time he saw it made him want to kiss her. But he saw what he wanted to see, just as his family told him. He had a blind spot large enough to fly head over heels through. The men weren't admiring her. They were fantasizing about fucking her.

Yes, she was impetuous. He knew that. Only a fool could have been blind to it. But her impulsiveness intrigued him, made him feel young again as he let her lead him into places that on his own he would not have gone. The trips to Mexican beaches. The spontaneous sex that erupted unexpectedly when they were doing something else, like walking in a park or when he would awake to find her humping him, her conjuring an erection even while he was asleep. There was never anything like it in his more or less button-downed life. And then, just as he had started throwing off the shackles of his self-restraint she changed, turning into the woman his sister had warned him about.

Things went haywire. The criticism only increased as one of his brothers started to flirt with her at family gatherings and she did nothing to stop it. She was just trying to be friendly, she told him. And he took her at her word until his sister told him the truth, that she had seen her and the brother fondling each other at Thanksgiving.

He saw it as a continuation of his family's initial misgivings. Yes, he saw her touching her brother's knee while at the table. But she was only laughing at something he'd said. Others were laughing, too. It was only a coincidence that they sat next to each other. But then came Christmas and for the first time she was the one who insisted on spending the holiday with his family. It was the middle year of their brief marriage. Far too early, he believed, to be infected with infidelity. But he misjudged her concupiscence for playfulness and when he finally saw it for himself on New Year's Eve—the two of them, his brother and his wife, fucking in his old room upstairs in his parents' house, the bed covered with coats, her seeing him but ignoring him as if to say he would be next in line, as if she could not resist her own impulse—he felt a rage rise in him that, had he been a less rational man, might have ended up as a double murder and possible suicide.

But he was not that kind of man.

He was the kind of man to pull his leather bomber's jacket out from under her naked ass, which she raised just enough to accommodate him without spoiling her moment, his oblivious brother, his face red as a pimple, humping her nonstop. It was all too much for Jacob as he stumbled down the narrow, carpeted stairway shrieking, "Fuck you, fuck all of you," and fleeing into the cold dark night to his car, his head throbbing with a rage that only a thick skull could contain.

"Fuck you, fuck everybody," he shouted at the brightly lit fifties Cape Cod house as if it were listening, blindly racing down the snowy street, one block, two blocks, three blocks past a stop sign, plowing into a snowbank that only partially cushioned the car as the front end slammed into a telephone pole, causing it to sway like the pine tree it had once been.

2

By the turn of the century, his marriage behind him, Jacob fell into a series of increasingly lucrative jobs, first rewriting code to prepare for the Year 2000 transition and then as part of a team creating a complex financial tracking system for a state agency. Both positions resulted in hundreds of hours of overtime. This lasted until a new administration shut down the project when it became apparent that it would never be finished. However, by his own frugal standards, he'd saved enough to last the rest of his life. If only he could decide what to do with his life. Having burned out as a programmer, and with the memory of his devastating divorce fresh in his mind, he longed for solitude. He had come to despise the unrelenting noisiness of city life, the thousands of small compromises one had to make to live what others called a normal life. He found himself gravitating toward solitary hikes in the north woods, sometimes driving many miles to places where few visited where he found comfort in the rugged beauty.

It was during one of his hikes that he came upon a dilap- idated shack. The door hung askew by a single hinge, the rough-hewn boards failing to properly stiffen the rickety frame and its sagging roof. The inside, musty and dark, revealed the remains of a mattress, a rusting cookstove and a pile of moldy clothes. It appeared nobody had lived there for years.

From its position in a small clearing overlooking the tributary, he could see cabins on the other side of a beaver pond. The cabins, sided with clapboards, were elevated on pilings above a gentle slope leading to the pond. Surrounded by a pine forest that blocked out much of the sun, a narrow dirt road disappeared behind a rise that formed a backdrop to the cabins. As far as he could tell, he was the only person there.

He sat on the ridge for a long time, listening to the subtle crackling of leaves and twigs that advertised the comings and goings of wildlife and the chirping and calls of birds, mostly cardinals and noisy blue jays. It was late spring and where the sun reached he saw wildflowers and shrubbery in many shades of green. Above him, the parallaxing pines swayed in a gentle breeze that didn't reach the ground. The peace he felt was a revelation. This is the kind of place he was looking for and, as it turned out, it was for sale.

Behind the shack he followed a narrow, overgrown trail that led to a dirt road embedded with gravel, and among the bullet-pocked Posted signs was a rusted FOR SALE sign with a phone number. He entered the number on his cell phone's contact list and then he did something impulsive. He pulled the sign down and tossed it into the woods. He would call the number when he got home, hoping that the property was still on the market.

3

THE SALESMAN WONDERED WHY ANYONE WOULD WANT the property. It was difficult to reach, had no services, was located in a forest infested with Ixodes scapularis, commonly known as a deer tick, a vector for Lyme disease. But it had been on the market for years and he was happy to forward Jacob's lowball offer to the owner or rather the heirs of the owner, who wasted no time in accepting.

Over the next dozen years Jacob transformed the property into his home, first by paying a contractor to erect the shell of the five-hundred-square-foot cabin, which he finished on his own over the intervening years. A well was drilled, trees were felled to welcome more sunlight, followed by a modest array of photovoltaics and a small, seldom-used generator.

Over the years he'd met the neighbors as they came and went during their mostly summer vacations. They rarely stayed more than a week and sometimes their friends or relatives would use the cabins, almost never during the winter. One was strictly a rental that saw little use. The part-time neighbors waved to him as he paddled and drifted up and down the pond during the vacation months, waving back, almost always clothed in a long-sleeved khaki shirt and cargo shorts, his head covered by a kayaker's hat. Although he'd purchased the property to get away from people, he didn't mind the occasional intrusion, often engaging in the kind of small talk that eluded him in what he had come to view as his previous life. Even so, the quiet winter was his favorite season.

Despite how busy he was improving his property and doing the endless chores that went with maintaining it, he reserved plenty of time for exploration, often taking long hikes in the surrounding forest. He kept a kayak at the base of the ridge, just a few feet from the edge of the pond, which he would use to fish for bluegills, crappie and the accidental bass. On several occasions he portaged and paddled downstream to the Flambeau with its many rapids and wide, still passages framed by unsurpassed colors in the fall. But the return trip was always difficult, involving more portaging and taking much more time than the downstream trip. Eventually, he would load the kayak onto his pickup and drive to a landing, avoiding the arm and shoulder fatigue that tortured him during the long upstream slogs.

It didn't bother him that he had to hike to the road behind his property to get cell reception. And then it seemed to depend on the direction of the wind or the time of day. He'd avoided his family ever since that winter night. Something had clicked inside him that had wiped out any affection he'd previously felt for his siblings or his aging parents. And judging by the infrequency of any of them trying to contact him, the feeling was mutual. In the beginning, an email here and there popped up on his phone, to which he didn't respond. What was there to say? The humiliation of that moment clung to him like PTSD.

4

AN INVETERATE REMODELER WITH DECENT SKILLS, HE'D developed his estate over the years, turning nearby trees into firewood, adding a small workshop, a propane tank, and most of the comforts of home. He'd expanded the clearing, bringing in more light to his photovoltaics that provided sufficient charge to the battery backup system he'd installed to power the LEDs and chargers.

For a year or two, his relatives would mention him on their Myspace accounts, which he would occasionally read on his laptop when he was some place with an internet connection. Some of the cousins thought he was dead. His siblings insisted he was alive, referring to him as *estranged*. There was even a flurry of posts referring to acquaintances whose family members were similarly incommunicado, as if to normalize the behavior.

"They just don't get it," he would tell himself and, as if to convince himself, would run down his list of grievances aloud.

He talked to himself often during those early years. How else to get his thoughts out in the open? How else to work out problems, especially when working on projects? Most of the time, he asked himself questions and it seemed only natural that he would answer them aloud as well.

But he talked up a storm, occasionally resulting in a lengthy rant that produced a counter argument, like a debate between himself and another version of himself. Anyone watching this would think him crazy. He would think himself crazy. But he felt that it kept him sane, especially during the long winter months when he'd snowshoe and ski for miles and skate on the frozen pond after clearing enough snow to make a rink. But there was more than recreation involved. Three of the cabin owners paid him to keep an eye on their properties. He had their information in his contact list. Each had a different concern. One wanted to know if his place had burned down. Another was afraid that squatters would take over his property. The third was concerned about flooding, which was not an issue during the winter but could happen in the spring, especially if the beavers enlarged their dam.

Jacob thought he was stealing their money, as none of the things the owners feared happened. There were no floods because each spring he would clear parts of the dam to prevent it. None of the cabins was consumed by fire. And the location was so remote that no squatter would find it. Which made it all the more unusual when on a bright, mid-January morning a steady stream of gray smoke wafted from the stovepipe of the cabin farthest from his property.

5

THIS WAS ONLY THE THIRD TIME ANYONE HAD occupied one of the cabins during the winter. The first time, the family had come out to spend Christmas in the woods. He recalled talking to the owner who complained about how difficult it had been to get his car up the frozen, unplowed road and how he'd never do it again for fear of sliding into a ravine. The second time, the owner of the fourth cabin, the one farthest from Jacob's home, had come out with a group of friends to celebrate the New Year in a big way, lighting up the starry sky with fireworks. And this time when he put his binoculars on the cabin he made note of two dark-colored SUVs parked above it on the hillside, just off the road.

Should he check it out? He didn't recognize the cars but it was difficult to make out details through the obscuring trees. Should he call the owner? And thus the internal debate began. It wasn't what he was paid to do. All the owner wanted to know was whether his place had burned down. Jacob had asked him whether he was concerned about other things, such as squatters. But the man laughed dismissively, which annoyed Jacob. He'd watch it from his property, but for the moment he decided not to pay it more attention. The man said he was concerned about fire, not visitors, not smoke coming from the stovepipe.

However, like someone trying to not scratch an itch, he couldn't ignore it, periodically putting the glass on the cabin, noticing that the occupants had stamped out foot-paths all around the place, as if marking their territory. Several times he looked at the contact list on his phone but refrained from calling. He had an aversion to phone conver-sations to begin with, and it didn't bother him that reception was spotty at best. It just gave him an excuse not to make a call.

Was it odd for a loner to prefer face-to-face conversa-tions? He didn't enjoy having other people around, yet he liked to talk, which was made obvious by the conversations he held with himself. As the years passed he often made a point of paddling past the cabins when people were around, asking how they were, responding to their questions, which usually had to do with his predictions for the weather, as if he were a meteorologist, and whether the county was ever going to fix their road. How many times could he tell them it was a logging road? How many times would they need to ask? But it was a meaningless face-to-face conversation and for whatever reason he got joy from it.

But in the dead of winter? He couldn't just noncha-lantly paddle to the cabin as if he were just passing by. They weren't spending time outside in the snow. They were inside doing whatever it was and the thought of hiking over there and banging on the door just to see what was going on seemed unnatural, invasive. So he let it ride. He valued his own privacy too much to invade someone else's. He might check them out tomorrow, if they were still there.

6

JACOB DIDN'T KNOW WHAT TO THINK WHEN THE NEXT morning he woke to sporadic gunfire. No stranger to firearms, he knew it when he heard it. Hunting season was over. Snow had fallen overnight and the temperature was in the low twenties. He dressed hurriedly, throwing on a navy blue cable knit sweater, sweat pants and thick wool socks which he squeezed into a pair of hiking boots that he didn't bother to lace. Grabbing his binoculars, he stepped gingerly outside to investigate. The shots were coming from near the cabin, two people shooting at what? He couldn't tell. Target practice? he wondered. Seemed too cold for that but maybe they were city folk bent on firing a few rounds. Both were bundled in parkas, clouds of steam filling the still air with every breath.

But he was wary. Now that he had seen their faces, he was certain neither one was the cabin's owner, though he might be inside. Worse, they seemed to be firing in different directions, across the pond, down its length and into the woods. Looking back at his cabin, smoke drifting from the stovepipe but breaking up quickly as it worked its way into nearby trees, he wondered if they realized they weren't alone. At least they weren't aiming at the ridge line. Briefly, he thought about waving to them, making his presence known in a friendly way, but it brought up an uneasiness that he could not dismiss. He'd keep an eye on them for now as he returned to his cabin, hoping that his cabin, which was out of view from where the men were shooting, would remain that way.

But it was hard for him not to think the worst. The gunfire had unnerved him. Strangers with guns unnerved him. He thought about calling the owner, even took out his phone and scrolled through his contacts. But he couldn't bring himself to do it, in the unlikely event he could conjure up a signal. What would he say? The fact that he seldom used his phone imbued every call with added significance. He'd lived alone in the woods for so long that anything from outside was an intrusion, an invasion of his privacy, a potential threat. Sometimes it made his hands sweat. And then he thought about what they would think, a stranger to them as much as they were strangers to him, were he to strap on his snowshoes and show up at their front doorstep. Would they welcome him, or would they point their guns at him? One thing was for sure, he'd bring his Glock 19 with him, concealed, of course. Just in case.

THE GUNFIRE ENDED NOT LONG AFTER JACOB HAD returned to his cabin, and for the rest of the day men went in and out, stomping a path in the dirty snow leading to the vehicles. For his part, Jacob left his cabin several times, moving stealthily through the woods to get a better view of the comings and goings, certain that he couldn't be seen, catching glimpses of them only once. Between his forays, he cleaned his guns: the Glock, the 12-gauge and the Winchester Model 70 deer rifle.

It can't hurt to call, he finally said, to himself. Loudly. The activity had stopped by mid-afternoon just as the morning sun was crowded out by an encompassing whitish-gray overcast from which snow was beginning to fall. A TV meteorologist had warned of another six to twelve inches that could blanket northwestern Wisconsin. Traveler advisories were issued. Being snowed in didn't bother him. He knew what cabin fever was but had never suffered from it. He always had something to do, something to keep him busy, something to get him through the long nights.

Apparently, the visitors didn't feel the same way. Sometime during the afternoon the cars had been driven away, though Jacob hadn't seen nor heard them. He'd noticed they were gone just before dark, on his final patrol of the day. Watchful waiting had worked again. Doing nothing turned out to be the best course of action, once again. So many times things just got better on their own if one just let things be. Relieved that he didn't have to make a phone call, he returned to his cabin, put another log in the wood stove and relaxed in his recliner with a shot of schnapps, a glass of brandy and the unreliable reception of satellite TV to keep him company.

LIGHT SNOW WAS FALLING INTERMITTENTLY AS JACOB sipped his first cup of coffee of the day. Looking out the small front window, he could see that a foot of snow had fallen overnight. The thick overcast told him it wasn't going to let up anytime soon.

To satisfy his curiosity, he stepped into the impossibly white powder wearing only his moccasin slippers, socks, sweatpants and long-sleeved undershirt to see if the visitors had returned, hoping that they hadn't. The air was frosty and dry. He needed his binoculars to penetrate the curtain of falling snow to determine that the cars hadn't returned.

Smiling contentedly, he high-stepped his way to his cabin for a breakfast of pancakes and maple syrup. His appetite appeased, he geared up with snowpants, boots, parka and sunglasses and carefully made his descent from the ridge to the pond thirty feet below. No point in taking a weapon, he'd decided. The men were gone and the neighborhood was his alone.

Sliding like a child across patches of ice where the powdery snow had not stuck, he approached the cabin in no hurry, propelled by little more than his curiosity. He often did this when the vacationers came and went in the summer. Just to check things out. People sometimes left things behind. But not this time. They hadn't shuttered the windows like the other cabins. That's usually what people did before leaving for good. Did it mean they were coming back? He slowed his pace, his steps becoming deliberate. No more sliding on the ice. It hadn't occurred to him yet that with every step he was leaving a trail that led directly to his cabin. He was still more curious than concerned.

The blinds were drawn on the front window. Like the other cabins, it was raised two feet above the ground on concrete blocks, which put the window sill at eye level for him. Doubtful that he would be able to see anything, he nonetheless drew up to the window. The bottom rail of the blinds rested firmly on the sill but the lowest slat had failed to close, leaving enough of an opening for Jacob to squint into the dim interior. A moment passed as he cupped his hands around his eyes to block out the daylight. Snow fell quietly in the stillness. And then he staggered back from the cabin as if he'd been punched.

9

Now he wished he'd brought a gun. Rattled, he crouched as if to make himself smaller, anxiously scanning the terrain as if someone were hidden behind a tree, watching or taking aim. His instinct was to run, but he hesitated. Had he seen what he thought he'd seen? Standing in the snow facing the cabin, he stood out, a ready target. Removing a glove, he took out his phone, dropping it in the snow. Brushing it off, he saw that there was no signal. Not surprising. That's how it usually was in his neighborhood. The surge of fear that had enveloped him dissipated as he fat-fingered his way to the camera app. He needed proof, a photo. Quickly returning to the window, he pressed the phone against the glass and fired off several frames. Nothing there. Then he fired several more, this time with the flash. The result was worse. He struggled with the reflections.

Pressing his face against the window, his eyes lined up with the gap between the slats, he held this position until he was certain that his eyes hadn't deceived him. He tried the door. It wouldn't budge. He was exposed and alone and quickly turned tail, picking up speed with every step until reaching the base of the ridge, his heart racing, sweat pouring. Clambering up the slippery, steep hill, he looked back at the snow-covered pond, bright even without the sun, his footsteps clearly visible, like a dotted line on a map connecting his cabin with the place he'd fled.

What if they came back? he wondered as he reached his cabin.

The first thing he did was to grab his pistol, chamber a round and flick the safety. Then he stepped out to glass the area around the cabin. The parking area was still empty. But he feared it would only be a matter of time before they returned. His only option was to scramble to higher ground, up to the top of the ridge where he had parked his pickup alongside the snowed-in service road. It emptied onto a county road. Not having been driven for more than a week, his truck was encased in snowdrifts and ice. Even with four-wheel drive he didn't see how he could drive through the snow. He checked his phone. Still no signal.

Moving on, he found himself in deep snow and wishing he'd brought his snowshoes. But he stomped and clomped to a clearing near the high point of the ridge and there, as he held his phone in his bare hands and waved it slowly like a wand, two bars appeared on the screen. He poked at the keypad and held the phone to his ear.

A woman's practiced voice announced, "911. What is your emergency?"

"I THINK THERE'S BEEN A MURDER," HE SAID excitedly.

"What's your name, sir?"

"Jacob Alexander. I think I saw a body in one of the cabins."

"Do you have GPS, sir?"

"I live off a logging road near Bear Creek. But we're off County Road M."

"Are there others with you?"

"No."

"You said we're."

"I meant .... There's cabins across from me. It's one of those cabins. I saw someone in one of them. He was tied up in a chair and it looked like he was bloody. He was kinda slumped. And it looked like there was someone else on the floor. I thought I could see shoes, but I'm not sure."

"But you're sure you saw a person in a chair who was tied up?"

"Yes, yes, that's what I saw. I tried to get a picture but couldn't. Please send someone out. They might come back."

There was a slight pause.

"Who might come back?"

"The people who did this. They're gone now but they've been here a coupla days. They were out shooting rifles the other day. I never thought—"

"Sir," she said, cutting him off, "we have your approximate location."

"Great."

"Unfortunately, there aren't many towers so when I say approximate, it could be several miles off from where you actually are. Is there any way you can drive to meet a deputy?"

Jacob hesitated before responding.

"I don't think so."

"Can you tell me where the logging road intersects with M?"

Jacob racked his brain but his mental map didn't include labels for roads, just that they were there. And he knew it wasn't a single logging road and he could not explain which branch to take to get to his place. He was aware of the tradeoffs of isolation and he'd accepted them. Of course, he'd never expected to see the mess in the cabin. He'd driven the road that led to the cabins on the other side of the creek, but that was years ago, and he didn't think he could do it again from memory.

He couldn't think of any landmarks at the intersection with the county road. Not even nearby. It wound through ubiquitous forest and he'd driven it so often that he didn't even think about it when he was behind the wheel. But now, standing in the deep snow, he felt confused. He hit a wall when it came to helping the woman locate him.

"Maybe I can hike down to M," he said, finally. "It's a

couple of miles but I can go back and get my skis and maybe get down there faster."

"Really? You can ski there?"

"Well, sort of. For the downhill parts."

"You don't have a snowmobile?"

The signal wavered.

"I do but it's got problems..."

"That's okay, sir," the woman said reassuringly, as the signal started to break up. "We'll get someone on the way. If you can think of something that might help us get to you, please..."

"What should I do if they come back?" he said into dead air.

11

After several tries, Jacob gave up on reestablishing the signal. Returning to his cabin, he grabbed his binoculars for a thorough inspection of the valley, the pond and the cabins. He wished for a means to erase the trail he had left on the ice. His mind raced. He thought he was in a decent defensive position should they return. He had a clear view and the only way they could attack him without his being aware of it would be if they came from behind, which he didn't believe they were equipped to do. He was confident that he would either see them or hear them long before they'd get a bead on him. He told himself it would be up to him whether he fought or fled.

His anxiety dissipated with time and he felt that he was back in control. The options played out in his head. He could stay where he was and wait for the deputies to arrive. How they would get from the county road to the cabins without snowmobiles or a helicopter was a puzzle. He didn't think they had a chopper. How likely would they trailer a snowmobile? He had no idea. And then there was the remoteness. The location on either side of the pond existed only because of a maze of old logging roads that zigzagged erratically through the woods. A left turn here, a right turn there, and all of a sudden you were lost.

What if the killers had snowmobiles? He hadn't seen any, but that didn't mean they didn't have them. What if they dismounted their snowmobiles far enough from his cabin that he couldn't hear them? They could sneak up and surprise him from the rear. Suddenly, he was not so certain he could fend them off. Having no experience with such a threat, he began to think it best if he hiked out to meet the deputies down below on the county road. But what were the odds that he'd be there just when they drove by? He would just be wondering whether he'd missed them or whether they had yet to drive by.

Satellite internet was too expensive and unreliable in the woods. He'd tried it and found it to be as dependable as satellite TV. It worked on clear days but often couldn't find a signal through overcast, rain or snow. Satellite internet was much slower than wired or wireless and there were times when it just stopped working. Even the wind seemed to throw it off. Reception on his small flatscreen had always been twitchy. He'd relocated the dish multiple times over the years but somehow it didn't seem to matter. Sometimes it worked, and sometimes it didn't. Just like his phone. He wondered how much more snow was on the way. Clouds had been rolling and the sky was thick with them. Even so, he left the TV on, its screen filled with broken images, expecting that eventually the signal would return. He was hoping for a weather update.

The temperature was in the mid-twenties, the wind almost imperceptible, and looking out the window he could see the white stuff starting to pick up.

"You want to know what the weather is," he mumbled, "just look out the window."

12

It wasn't long before snow began to fall in earnest, slowly filling the tracks he'd left on the pond. Another hour or two of this, he thought, and no one would know he'd been there. At a certain point he stopped monitoring the cabin and started wondering whether the police were coming. Perhaps they thought he was a crank caller. Maybe they couldn't find the logging roads under the snow. He was losing his patience with watchful waiting. It only seemed to stoke his anxious imagination. He felt a need to do something, anything to make it seem like he was in control.

He could either go down to the cabin, break in and document what he believed to be a crime scene, or try to intercept the sheriff. The first option was silly and dangerous, he decided. Why reveal himself if they came back? He had decent cross country skis and knew of shortcuts that revealed themselves in deep snow. The logging road behind his cabin, even with several feet of snow, wasn't as direct as following the ridge, which extended a mile and while not all downhill, could be traversed without the need for snowshoes. Certainly it would be physically challenging to maintain his stride and there would be places where he might have to remove his skis, but it would be faster than walking in snowshoes, which could be exhausting work.

Dressing quickly, he knew he'd start sweating almost from the start. He had to dress lightly enough to minimize the sweat and heavily enough to minimize the cold. But he figured he would reach the road in an hour, if everything went according to plan and the shortcuts he had in mind actually existed. It's not as if he hadn't done this type of skiing before, just that he hadn't done it with heavy snow falling. He knew there was a risk that blizzard conditions could arise, that he could get disoriented in a whiteout and that he couldn't carry enough gear to satisfy all conditions. And he hoped that, once he made it to the road, he'd be able to ride with the deputy, as the return trip would be mostly uphill.

He filled a bright green daypack with water bottles, snackbars, a lightweight emergency blanket that he'd never used but hoped would work if he ended up spending the night in the snow, an LED headlamp, rope, handwarmer, extra pair of socks, and two magazines for the nine mil, which he holstered. In his pants pocket were a butane lighter, compass and three and a half inch pocket knife. He hoped he had enough to sustain him as he stepped out the back door, walking to the snow-covered road where he stepped into his skis and, with poles in each hand, pushed his way forward.

Deputy Carson Pennington had an idea where the cabins were. A very general idea. He'd hiked and driven the back roads of northwestern Wisconsin for much of his twenty-eight years. He was familiar with the iffyness of abandoned logging roads, how you could suddenly end up in a ditch, or careen over a bluff. He was aware of the uneven snowfall that had hit the county and how it had stopped for a while and now was coming down with intensity. The dispatcher had told him about the 10-54 and that it ended abruptly and the 911 operator was unable to reestablish the connection. Nobody was surprised. That's the way it was with cell phones in the woods.

Seeing how snowed-in the landscape was, he was skeptical about being of any help. Rural driveways, many of them leading to unoccupied seasonal homes, were caked with old and new snow that awaited plowing. Unsurprisingly, the dispatcher was unable to provide an accurate location based on cell tower triangulation. The fact that she had received a call from someone deep in the forest was unusual. All that Pennington had been told was that the caller lived off County Road M near a logging road on Bear Creek. However, neither the logging roads or Bear Creek were on the county map. But he knew of one section along the road that had been logged years ago that had since regrown. The caller lived somewhere in that part of the woods and apparently could drive to County Road M, though not after heavy snow. That meant that some of the logging roads were still usable, though he had no idea as to which ones, and with the heavy snow it might be impossible to tell just by looking.

Without precise information, he drove up and down a five-mile section of the road several times. A snowplow had passed recently, which made his job a little easier. There was little traffic this early in the morning so it didn't matter that he slowed to a crawl, scanning the snowy forest for the caller.

It was his first 10-54, signifying a possible dead body. While the thought of finding bodies energized him, he hated having to drive up and down the road, seeing the same things with no suggestion he would succeed in his mission. If only he had a snowmobile. But he didn't. All he had were snowshoes in the trunk. His uniform was not conducive to hiking in the woods, lacking ventilation, meaning that even on a short hike in the woods he'd be soaked with sweat. The only relief would come by unfastening his duty parka, letting some of the heat out while letting the cold air in. He couldn't decide which was worse, hot sweat or cold sweat. Hiking in the woods off the job, he would have worn lighter weight, layered clothing, underclothes that wicked sweat from the skin and insulated hiking boots instead of the department-issued toe crunchers that worked well on pavement but not for hikes in the snow.

Getting back on the road, about midway between the

two endposts of his circuit, he saw headlights in the distance, approaching from the opposite direction, falling snow obscuring a clear view. He wondered if they were locals and, if they were, whether they could help him find the cabins the caller had talked about. Putting his car in idle near one of the snowed-in access roads, he waited.

A pair of distant headlights turned into two pairs as the vehicles approached, one behind the other. He turned on his roof lights.

JACOB ENJOYED CROSS COUNTRY SKIING, BUT HE HAD his limits. He didn't like the idea of destinations. He just liked to get out in the woods and travel over terrain that during other seasons was covered with rotting logs, stumps, vines and debris that a sensible person such as himself would avoid. Since there weren't any trails, he had to make his own way, slowly at first as he settled into a comfortable stride, skiing on the diagonal on gentle rises and side-stepping on the slopes that required it. The reward for side-stepping was the prospect of a short downhill run on the other side, though even then he couldn't go full bore for fear of hitting a tree or stump.

Stopping often to reconnoiter using his compass, he kept himself on a bearing that he expected to lead him to CR-M. He'd thought about simply following the logging roads but it wasn't as if, buried in snow, they looked much different from the surrounding woods. The roads, such as they were, were narrow, barely able to fit a full-size pickup without vegetation scratching the paint. Besides, there wasn't a straight mile if you added them all together, and men who cut the roads had no concern for those who would use them.

Not a sports skier, he did not work on conditioning and only strapped on the skis when the urge struck, usually after a snowfall. Even though he'd spent his entire life in Wisconsin, he had little affection for the cold. No matter how prepared he thought he was, and he put great stock in layering of clothing, the longer he was out, eventually the cold and wet got to him and then he'd be wishing that he was back in his cabin in front of the cast-iron stove.

Jacob was elated when he reached a steep bluff overlooking CR-M. And tired. Already he felt soreness in his joints. While he couldn't see the car, he saw flashing lights from down the road.

"This is great," he said into the enveloping silence, immediately turning his attention to finding his way to the road. The descent looked too steep for skis, so he took them off. Should he take them with him or leave them? Hoping that the deputy or deputies would have a snowmobile, he hadn't planned to return the way he had come. Feeling fatigued, he didn't want to think of the prospect. But he'd need his hands to get to the bottom. So, he tied the skis and poles together with rope that he attached to his belt with a carabiner.

Halfway down, he could hear indistinct voices from the road.

"Hell, yeah," he muttered. It couldn't have worked out better for his aching body.

PENNINGTON HAD HOPED THE TRAVELERS WOULD BE locals but as he stepped out of his car, pulling up the hood of his parka to keep the snow from melting on his wavy hair, he saw that the cars had Michigan plates.

The young deputy held up his hand as he approached the middle of the two-lane asphalt road. For an instant it looked like the cars were going to blow past him but then they slowed before coming to an abrupt stop. Pennington had his eyes on the lead vehicle and didn't see that a passenger in the second car had stepped out, fiddling with something while running toward him.

He'd never felt anything like it as the buckshot exploded through his body, lacerating his internal organs, pellets pinging against his car. It was like being hit by a concrete block that pushed him back against his vehicle just as a second round turned his face into a bloody mask of dripping tissue. If there was pain, it didn't last long.

Four men quickly approached, standing over the deputy.

"What the fuck did you do, private?" the passenger of the lead car shouted.

The man with the shotgun shrugged.

"I thought that was what I was 'sposed to do, major, sir," the shooter said.

The major was livid. Older, larger, more powerfully built, he pushed the slender, twentyish shooter until he had him backed up against one of the SUVs, spewing angrily. This went on until the major's driver interrupted, taking the major aside.

"We don't have time for this, Wiley," he whispered. "We need to get a move on. You can deal with this later."

Anger was fixed on the major's face. But he recovered quickly, nodding in agreement.

"Is he dead?" he asked.

"Yeah, he's dead."

They worked methodically, gingerly stuffing the deputy's body into the backseat so as not to get blood and bits of flesh on themselves. His feet stuck out the door opening. One of them slammed the door several times but couldn't close it.

"What the fuck are you doing, Benny?" the major asked heatedly.

"I just thought it would look neater."

"What the fuck is wrong with you? He's fucking dead."

Stepping away from the car, three of them talked briefly while Benny popped the trunk. The conversation was animated as the leader continued to argue with the young man who'd killed the deputy.

"Should we take his guns?" Benny asked, peering into the trunk.

"Leave 'em," the major said. "Somebody get his radio. Hey, Benny, stop wasting time and get over here."

Benny hurried from the car.

"What's in the trunk?"

"A bunch of shit. Big first aid kit. Blanket, shit like that."

"Did you see any newspaper or a rag?" the leader said.

"There's a newspaper on the front seat," Benny said.

"Good, go get it," the major said.

"What for?"

"Just get it, okay?"

The major crumpled and rolled the two outermost sheets and handed it to the shooter.

"Do you think you can handle this, private?"

"Handle what?"

"Pour some gas on it. Use the can in my car."

"I get it," the shooter said, grinning. "Gonna blow it up, huh?"

This brought a knowing smile to Benny's face, as if he'd done this before.

The major and his driver returned to their vehicle and quickly pulled away. Benny watched from the driver's seat of the second car, revving the engine while the shooter prepared to blow up the police car. Igniting the newsprint with a butane lighter, the shooter ran to the SUV as Benny stepped on the accelerator, fishtailing down the icy road. Both cars stopped several hundred yards away near a bend in the road as a fireball erupted behind them.

16

THE GUNFIRE STARTLED JACOB AS THE WEIGHT OF HIS skis pulled on him, seeking out the quickest path to the bottom. Freezing in his descent, gripped by fear, he struggled to hold his place. The slope was slippery, and just beneath the snow a tangle of vines and roots waited to trap his feet. It didn't help that under the snow a blanket of leaves acted like a lubricant against his boots. His instinct was to pull out his handgun, but he resisted the impulse momentarily and instead sought protection behind a tree, flattening against the side of the slope, trying to make himself invisible in the snow. He could hear voices but couldn't make out the words. One of them sounded angry. While his mind raced to explain what was happening he removed his right glove and pulled his handgun from its holster, holding it in front of him, careful to release the safety silently. There was no question that something bad had happened, which became clear when a black SUV accelerated past him, raising a snowy blizzard in its wake, followed momentarily by a second car.

Immediately, he realized they were the same cars that

were parked at the cabin. And then they stopped, maybe a hundred yards from where he lay. Had they seen him? A shiver ran down his neck as he watched the cars from his prone position behind the tree. Suddenly the ground shook and an immense fireball lit up the road beneath him, the unexpected explosion hurting his ears. He was close enough to feel heat though he could not see what had exploded. In a matter of seconds, debris landed on hard surfaces, sounding like pieces of metal and glass. Stunned by the explosion, he'd momentarily forgotten about the two SUVs, which, when he looked back in their direction, had made their way around a bend in the road and were no longer in sight.

Maintaining his position momentarily, he tried to figure out what had happened and what, if anything, he should do about it. His mind raced, struggling to come up with an explanation. But his curiosity took the lead and he slipped and slid the remaining distance, winding up in a seated position in a snowdrift alongside the road. Detaching the carabiner, he left his skis and warily stepped into the center of the road where he got his first view of the blackened car, parts strewn across the road, flames jetting from its engine compartment, clouds of black smoke billowing. Approaching the flaming wreck cautiously, he saw what looked like a body amidst the ruins. It was obvious that it was a sheriff's car and the body was the deputy who had been sent out to investigate.

He tried his cell phone but couldn't get a signal. There was nothing he could do for the deputy. Nervously, he looked down the road, half expecting the SUVs to return. Acutely aware of his vulnerability, he told himself to get to higher ground, see if he could make a call. The soreness and fatigue he'd felt when he arrived at the steep bluff vanished as hormones saturated his veins. Retracing his path, pulling his skis behind him, he waved his phone in the air, moving from one clearing to another to no effect. At one point he stood over the wreckage, some fifty feet above it and used his phone to snap photos. But he didn't linger.

His mind started to build a narrative. He was now certain that the people who killed the deputy were responsible for the bodies in the cabin. They must be coming back for whatever reason. He couldn't decide whether to head back to his cabin or return to the road in hopes of flagging down a passing motorist. It would be obvious to anyone driving by that something bad had happened, but would they think he was the perpetrator? What would he do if he drove by in that situation? A lone stranger on the road in proximity to a dead cop? He'd keep driving. And what if the killers returned and they saw him? The situation had that feel to it, of everything having gone wrong with no end in sight. He wished he had someone to talk to, someone who could help him make sense of it. Instead, having seen the bodies in the cabin and now the deputy, he was primed to think the worst.

One thing was for certain, he couldn't afford to spend the rest of the day thinking about it. The snow was intensifying. Already it was erasing the tracks left by his skis. And he was getting colder and he saw a breeze developing in the trees.

He needed to get back before things got worse.

Two cars were parked partially on the roadway near a snowed-in logging road on County Road M. They were about a mile west of a smoldering police car. Four men stood in a circle near the cars, one of them holding the deputy's handheld radio. They were engaged in a fervent conversation.

"We shoulda paid more attention to the weather," one of them said, surveying the deep snow covering the logging road. "Maybe we should just get outta here. Those police cars got GPS and Lojacks."

"Yeah, it won't be long before this place is crawling with cops."

The leader, Wiley Crawford, looked at his companions with disdain. Things had gone to shit so fast that he could barely comprehend it. There was no plan to kill a cop. The plan was to return to the cabin, finish what they had started, and get out of Dodge.

"I shouldn't have fucking listened to you, Benny," Crawford said bitterly. "You're the one who wanted to go to town."

"Who wants to spend a night with a coupla bodies?" Benny Altergott said defensively. "Besides, nobody said no. You didn't say no."

Crawford shook his head and turned to the youngest member of his crew, Tony Mumphrey.

"And you? What the fuck were you thinking? Offing a cop, for chrissakes."

Benny and the fourth member, Michael Gerlach, watched intently as the young killer faced Crawford.

Mumphrey shrugged, brushing the snow from the top of his buzz cut.

"If I ain't mistaken," Mumphrey said, "the guy in the cabin is a fed and Glen's a traitor? Am I right?"

"What's your point?"

"I figured we didn't want no fucking cop getting in the way. That's what the generals been saying, if I ain't mistaken."

"They were talking about infiltrators. Spies, not street cops," Benny said disparagingly.

"As far as we know, the fed is still alive," Crawford said. "At least he was. I didn't think we were finished with him, but now I'm not so sure. Even if he's dead, we coulda hid his body so nobody would find it, but now..."

"They don't know who we are," Mumphrey said, smiling. "Because of me."

"Unless the cop radioed in," Gerlach said.

Mumphrey glared at him.

"What I'm thinking is we either get lucky or get the hell outta here," Gerlach said. "I didn't sign up for no capital rap."

"Wisconsin don't have the death penalty, sergeant," Benny said.

"I didn't sign up for life in prison, either. I vote we get back to Michigan, right now, right away."

"You're not following the bread crumbs," Crawford said. "The feds have the death penalty."

"Oh, yeah. I wasn't thinking."

"So, you just wanna leave the evidence up there? Our fingerprints and DNA are all over the place. I told you when we left we were coming back," Crawford said.

"We shoulda took care of business before we left," Benny said.

Crawford scowled at the underweight shrimp in the black parka.

"Benny, it was your idea to leave. You didn't say anything about taking care of business before we left."

"Yeah, well, I didn't know about the snowstorm. Besides, you didn't say nothin' either. You can't blame it all on me. If it was such a big fucking deal, why didn't you say something?"

"This is getting us nowhere," Crawford said, frustrated. "We gotta get up there somehow. I don't care if we gotta walk."

"How much time you think we got?" Gerlach asked anxiously. "They're gonna see our cars, man, and then it's over."

Crawford stepped to the front of his car, struggling to find a solution. Even if they could hike to the cabin through the knee-deep snow, how could they hide the cars? Maybe Gerlach was right. Cut their losses, leave while they could. Maybe hole up somewhere until they could get back to the cabin and then finish up. But in the back of his mind was the apprehension that someone, the authorities in particular, would beat them to the cabin and he couldn't see himself waiting for the snow to melt.

"You know, major," Benny said, "maybe we could rent some snowmobiles and get up there that way."

"Where we gonna rent them?" Gerlach asked. "We don't know anything about this part of Wisconsin. Shit, I never been west of Milwaukee before."

"I don't know," Crawford responded petulantly. "I don't live here either."

"Maybe we should vote on it," Benny said guardedly. He knew from experience that Crawford liked to make decisions himself. But when he couldn't make a decision, he opened the door to democracy.

"Let me think about it," Crawford sighed.

18

Winter was Eric Larsen's favorite time of year. The ruddy-faced former high school linebacker had started working for the county at twenty-one. Over the years, he had worked a variety of positions, but his favorite was driving snow plows. With a perch high over the road he looked down on everything, giving him a commanding view and an inflated sense of self-importance. There were times when he'd see dozens of cars following him as he cleared the way on a county road, slow, methodical and necessary. Occasionally, he'd help people out, push snow out of their driveway so they could get out. Strictly speaking, it was a violation of county policy, but nobody was watching him out in the boondocks. He'd accept a gratuity if they forced it on him, but never more than a token amount. And he didn't always help. They'd have to give a good story, like they had a doctor's appointment or something urgent and important. It was easy to say no to people who just wanted to get out of the house. He'd just tell them it was against county policy and that would end the conversation.

Virtually all of CR-M needed plowing. Heavy snow

kept most people off the roads, making his job easier. Occasionally a car would appear behind him and he'd pull over a bit to let it pass, the lane in the opposite direction barely passable. With lighter snow, motorists often let their impatience get the better of them and take risks to get around him. Occasionally, he'd come across a stranded motorist. Some of the time he would stop to ask if the person needed help, even call dispatch to have a wrecker come out, but mostly he'd get out and help push the vehicle if that's all it took, but he would never use the truck. Too much risk of damage.

Rounding a bend, he could see the two westbound cars, parked halfway on the road. That looked odd to him. The snow on the narrow shoulder must have been too deep. Or they were worried about slipping into the drainage ditch. Still, it was an unusual place to park.

One man stood in front of the cars, waving as the big snowplow approached. Although he couldn't quite figure out why they had stopped, the closer he got the more frantically the man waved, stepping into the middle of the road, coming dangerously close to where the edge of the big blade would pass.

"What the fuck?" Eric said, slowing the vehicle, his eyes zeroing in on the man, rolling down his window as he came to a stop, his foot tapping the brake.

19

Jacob processed what he'd seen while retracing his steps to his cabin. Even though he'd spent less than fifteen minutes on the road, snow was already filling in his tracks. Skiing where he could, he tried to make it all the way without taking them off, preferring to herringbone his way up rises, giving up where lack of energy or the force of gravity stopped him. Every moment seemed important. Every step put distance between him and the crime scene, even though Jacob hadn't forgotten that another crime scene waited not far from his cabin. But he was glad that he hadn't arrived at the road five minutes earlier. If he'd seen the police car before he saw the SUVs, he would have been a goner. Or would he have been able to defend himself and the deputy? He would have liked to think so. But timing was everything, he thought, stopping to catch his breath, listening as engine noise emerged somewhere in the distance on the opposite side of the valley. It was a sound he heard only when he stopped to listen, folding back the hood of his parka. He could no longer hear it by the time he'd reached the halfway mark of his trek

No way they were going to get their cars up the road, he thought as he listened to the distant low-pitched whine that penetrated the forest's cold silence. It was because of the quiet that he could hear it, though he could only tell that it was coming from somewhere on the other side. Otherwise, it would be getting louder rather than diminishing, as if it were going in the opposite direction from his course. He was familiar with the logging roads that provided the only access into the forest. They zig-zagged all over the place. The way the roads twisted through the forest, sound could be muffled by trees and the up and down terrain so that, even though it could barely be heard, a turn here or there would be enough to make it seem the sound had burst through a wall and was suddenly full-blown, only to fade out on the next turn.

Reaching the top of the ridge that led to his cabin, he waved his cell phone above his head. He wasn't going to get much higher unless he climbed a tree. Coming upon a clearing, he spent several minutes walking in circles, as if performing a ritual to appease the cell phone gods. The most he got was one bar, not enough to make a call. The more time he spent, the more anxious he became, the more invested he was in the phone than in getting to his destination. It was like beachcombing on Lake Michigan when he was a kid, how difficult it was to break off a treasure hunt when there was always the chance that the perfect stone waited five minutes down the beach. Or, when he was lucky, a trilobyte. Hope was like that. The object of desire was just around the corner, the cell signal was just waiting for his phone to hit the right spot. And when it didn't, which was what usually happened, all the time spent in pursuit seemed like a waste. He could have been home sooner had he not stopped.

But he finally stopped searching for the elusive signal, not because of anything he was doing but because of the intrusion of engine noise. Either it was getting closer, or his ears were playing tricks on him. Or was it an acoustic anomaly? It was so distinct, he thought he could hear gears grinding, and then it died out. He stuffed the phone in his jacket pocket and picked up the pace, his skis and poles working in concert for the most part, not quite machinelike but not slowing him either, the skis following what remained of the tracks they'd left on the outbound trip.

20

THE SNOWPLOW DRIVER REALIZED QUICKLY THAT HE'D made a mistake. No sooner did he put the transmission into neutral than a second man leaped onto the running board of the passenger side, a wide grin on his skinny face, a pistol pressed against the window. For an instant he thought about putting it in gear but he knew he could never get up enough speed to get away. The guy on the running board would shoot him before he got out of first gear.

Both hands on the big steering wheel, his head lowered dejectedly, Eric Larsen knew he had stumbled into something but had no idea what it was. The two men were joined by two others and he watched as they parlayed alongside the cab, the man with the pistol pointing his gun at him several times, smiling as he did so, as if it were a joke. Though he'd never needed a gun on the job, Larsen would have carried one had the county allowed it. He believed in gun rights, renewed his hunting license every year, whether he needed it or not.

He watched them as they talked but couldn't make out what they were saying. Seeing their SUVs, he wondered why they would hijack a snowplow. Surely both cars didn't break down. And why in this place? It was in the middle of nowhere. But these thoughts weren't helping him make a plan, as if somehow he could jump out of the cab and disappear into the woods before one of them, maybe all four of them, pulled out their guns and put an end to his reality.

Somehow he had to calm himself. Sweat beaded on his ruddy forehead. He was gripping the wheel so hard that his hands started to ache. Somehow he had to convince himself he wasn't a dead man. Somehow he had to convince himself that he was in control.

But he hadn't entirely given up on escape. The doors were locked, he knew the road well enough that he thought he could slip below the level of the windshield, put the truck in gear and maybe, with luck, he could get into third or fourth gear and be on his way, radio to dispatch, alert the sheriff and somehow end the day alive. And if it worked out that way, he would never again go anywhere without a gun, he told himself angrily, not on the job nor off, and if they fired him for it so be it.

Focused on survival, he didn't notice when one of them motioned for him to get out of the cab. Then one of them pulled on the door. For an instant he considered enacting his plan but the guy was standing on the running board, rapping on the window.

"Come on out," the man said. "The major wants to talk."

21

EVEN THOUGH THERE WAS NO HEAT IN THE CABIN when Jacob returned, he tore off his outerwear as if it were on fire. His long underwear was soaked in sweat that started to freeze as soon as it was exposed to the cold air. For several minutes he stood naked in the dimness, lit only by the glow of the overcast sky entering the small windows. Drying himself with a bath towel, he raced to put on dry clothing as if someone were chasing him. It wasn't until he squeezed into his lightweight thermals and a pair of thick hiking socks that he took a deep breath and started to formulate a plan.

His mind was all over the map during the return trip, hovering over various topics, some of them having to do with putting one ski in front of the other and others riveted on the broader situation. Though he'd looked at it for only a few seconds, the blackened body in the burning patrol car put everything into perspective. The men from the cabin were very bad guys and he needed to do everything he could to protect himself. He laid his deer rifle on the table alongside his holstered nine mil, two magazines and one box of ammunition for each weapon, neither of them full. He dug out an old K-bar knife with sheaf that he'd found in the woods and laid it alongside the pistol. Out of the closet he pulled his winter camo jacket and pants. He hadn't worn them in years, but they were still in good shape.

Still in his underwear and socks, he emptied his daypack on the table. He'd eaten half of the snack bars and emptied the water bottles, but everything else, the headlamp and rope, were intact and ready for use. This is how he prepared for most of his hikes and outings. Lay everything out on the table, take inventory, take what he thought he would need and leave the rest. But he wasn't going anywhere. Not just yet.

Dressed in the camo pants, he laced his boots and slipped into the jacket, zipping it half way. He dawdled for a moment to decide whether to take the nine mil, pulling it out of the holster and putting in a jacket pocket with the safety on. He didn't think he'd need it but it was one of those things where it would be better to have it and not need it than need it and not have it. Grabbing the binoculars, he left through the back door and moved past the small clearing that surrounded his cabin into the woods overlooking the pond. The black and white camo patterns blended well with the dark gray leafless understory of mostly aspen and birch. Positioning himself in the thick of the shrubbery, he glassed the cabin. Snow had filled in everything. The footpath the killers had worn alongside the cabin to the parking area was long gone. He could hear nothing but the light breeze as it filtered through the trees.

But something was different. The front door was partially open.

22

Eric Larsen was as nervous as he'd ever been. And afraid. He couldn't stop his right foot from trembling as he stepped out of his cab to meet the major. Half-expecting to be killed, his eyes focused on his shoes, he thought about his wife. Would the county take care of her if he was killed in the line of duty? And why was one of them holding out his hand to him?

"I'm sorry if we scared you," Wiley Crawford said apologetically, shaking Larsen's hand. "But we really need your truck."

"You can have it," Eric mumbled.

The leader seemed amused.

"We need you to drive it. Our cabin is up through there," he said, pointing at the forest.

Larsen raised his head and looked toward where the major pointed.

"Can you do it?" Benny asked expectantly.

Larsen could see the outlines of the logging road, lined on either side by a mix of deciduous and conifer trees. The first question that came to mind was whether the plow blade was too wide for the road. He sensed that if he said he couldn't do it, that would be the end. Or they'd beat him. Either way, he didn't have a choice. Stepping toward the snow-covered logging road he sighted it as it rose steeply and then turned to the right, following a slightly rising ridge to the next bend where it disappeared into the woods. He'd have to keep the blade at a sharp angle to avoid encroaching trees. And he'd have to go slowly or he might end up in a ditch.

"I can do this," he nodded. "How far back you going?"

"A mile, maybe two," one of them said.

"Let's get going then," the major said. "Benny, you ride with mister ...?"

"Larsen. Eric Larsen."

"Mister Larsen. And take your walkie-talkie."

Larsen gave Crawford a puzzled look.

"Not you. Benny."

"Got it right here," Benny said, smiling, patting his coat pocket.

"One last thing," the major said to Larsen, holding out his hand. "Gimme your phone."

23

Not only was the cabin door half open, but Jacob could see the head of the man, still strapped to the chair, but on the floor. The man was using his head to pull the balky door open.

This threw a wrench into Jacob's evolving plan. He'd assumed the bodies in the cabin were dead, especially in view of the deputy's murder, but that no longer seemed to be the case. Clearly, at least one of them was alive. Jacob had done a lot of risky and stupid things in his life, but not since spending a month in bed with viral pneumonia had he come to grips with his own mortality, his vulnerability.

The disease came on quickly and it was fortunate that he had been in Madison to attend a kayak tradeshow. He remembered the profuse sweating and fever that at first he thought was some kind of flu. He woke exhausted the next morning, having gotten little sleep. But he had been looking forward to the show for months and was determined to go back the second day. He'd scouted the yaks the first day and had settled on one that was substantially lighter than his own. However, he couldn't stop coughing while waiting for the bus. Others at the bus stop shied away from him, it was so obvious. A woman asked if he was okay. He shook his head, coughing into his hand.

"You should see a doctor," she said.

Instead, he bought a bottle of the strongest cough syrup and returned to the hotel only to spend the night coughing up mucus. Thinking that it would be a relief to die, he spent another sleepless night before packing up and driving to a hospital where they told him that he was lucky to be alive.

If the woman hadn't planted the seed, would he have gone to the hospital the next morning? There was reason to doubt it. But it made him think about helping the man, who was obviously alive. He couldn't think of anything he'd done that anyone would call heroic. He was not the type to interfere in other people's business. He respected privacy, especially his privacy. It was why he took up residence in the woods.

His fear tamed momentarily by the obligation he felt to help the injured man, Jacob made a beeline down the snowy slope, one giant step after another, almost losing his balance before reaching level ground where he slowed to reconnoiter. There was no one in the woods. No sounds other than the breeze. He could see the man now, his shoulders across the door sill, worming his way onto the tiny porch.

"You okay, mister?" he asked timidly as he approached the cabin, as if not wanting to startle him.

The man strained to lift his head and groaned.

"I'll be right back," Jacob said reassuringly. "I'm gonna get you outta here."

24

"Goddammit, goddammit, goddammit," Jacob said aloud after returning to his cabin.

Why did he come back? He should have stayed on the road. Sooner or later the cops would come and he'd be safe. He could tell them what he knew, what he saw. Certainly, they wouldn't know that there were killers on the loose. Not immediately. He could've told them about the bodies in the cabin. But it was too late for that now. If only he could get his snowmobile to start. He'd have to take the long way down, but it would be faster than trudging through the snow, and he could load the man onto a sled and together they'd ride out of the woods to safety.

He'd tried to start it once this winter, after the first big snowfall. It blew huge clouds of blue smoke and sputtered. He'd started it repeatedly but it would stop after a few seconds. He wasn't a mechanic, but he'd searched online when he was in town and from the descriptions he'd read the problem was most likely the spark plugs, the fuel lines or the carburetor. At the time he didn't need the vehicle so he let things lie. Now he needed it but there was no time to fix it.

There had to be another way.

25

GETTING BEHIND THE WHEEL WAS A RELIEF TO LARSEN. They needed him to drive, he thought, as he buckled his shoulder harness. This became clear as soon as Benny took his seat on the passenger side of the cab.

"Boy, this is big, ain't it?" he said. "Man, we're high up, ain't we?"

Larsen nodded. His mind wasn't on the truck. He was calculating his chances with the hyperactive gunman. The man was on the small side, with a triangular face and the kind of close-cropped haircut popular with the military and prisoners. Seeing Larsen strap in, he fiddled with his shoulder belt, buckled it and removed it a moment later because it rested uncomfortably across his neck. Of course, the little guy had a gun, which he displayed, waving it as he settled into his seat just to make sure the driver knew who was boss. The other men remained on the road as Larsen adjusted the blade, eyeballing the depth. Given how quickly the logging road gained elevation, he wanted to have enough clearance so the bottom edge wouldn't dig into surface or worse strike a hidden boulder. Given that he couldn't see the road surface, he proceeded cautiously, inching forward at first.

It didn't take long for Benny to complain.

"This is boring," he said. "Can't you go faster? This is gonna take all day."

"You want to roll down the side of the hill?"

Benny looked out the window, pressing his face against the glass. The slope on his side of the road seemed to drop out from under the truck.

"You don't think we're too close to the edge?"

"We're right where we need to be."

While responding rotely to his passenger's comments, Larsen began to think that he could disable him with a well-placed blow to his throat. But what would happen to the gun? Would he drop it on the floor? Would Larsen be able to secure it before Benny recovered? One thing that worked in his favor was that the other men couldn't see more than the top of his head from the road and Benny, being smaller, was hidden by the seat back.

Despite his plan to move slowly, the plow easily pushed aside the uncompacted snow but the steep slope made it difficult to see the road in front of him, which unnerved Benny.

"Are you sure we're on the road?" he asked anxiously, leaning forward but seeing only the ample yellow hood.

The side mirror gave the driver a clear view of the other gang members, who were leaning against their cars, watching. He could incapacitate Benny and they would never know it. What would he do then? He'd have to kill Benny. He could not afford to deal with him and his companions simultaneously. He wondered whether he could do it. Point the gun at him and pull the trigger before having a second thought. He wasn't certain whether his companions would hear the gunshot, what with the diesel noise and distance. If he was lucky, they wouldn't hear it. That might give him enough time to escape.

Once he reached the top of the incline and angled to the right, he'd be able to make speed until it jogged to the left again. But that was as far as he could see. He had no idea what lay beyond. As far as his GPS was concerned, the road didn't exist. If he was going to do something, it had to be now.

But as if Benny could hear Larsen's thoughts, he pressed his back against the passenger door, pointing the gun at the driver.

"I know what you're thinking," he said matter-of-factly. "Just keep driving. No funny stuff."

Larsen's chest heaved as he inhaled deeply, his hands gripping the wheel, helplessness and anger colliding irresistibly. The urge to strike was so strong that he could barely restrain it. But with the pistol pointed at his abdomen he couldn't risk it. He had to bide his time. But he couldn't let Benny have the last word.

"What are you gonna do? Shoot me? Here, you wanna drive, take the wheel."

In a final defiant gesture, Larsen lifted his hands from the wheel.

"Go ahead. I'm a dead man anyway."

26

The sled was a black polyethylene tub with molded runners on the flat bottom. Jacob had most recently used it to haul firewood. Weighing about fifteen pounds, it was easy to pull on flat surfaces with a full load, but was problematic on slopes. Often, this meant he sought easier routes, which were usually much longer. There was no question that he would have taken the long way to the pond had he been out collecting firewood, but the urgency of the situation led him to take the most direct route, down the steep embankment between his cabin and the pond. He hoped the tub wouldn't have a mind of its own and dump its contents on the way down. But the descent would save time and allow him to arrive at his destination quickly with its load of blankets and pillows.

His deer rifle slung across his shoulder, his pistol on his hip, he had kept the sled on track and, reaching the bottom, he reassured himself that the killers were nowhere in sight, though he thought he heard a truck somewhere in the woods. The man in the cabin had continued to crawl onto the ice-covered pond, his legs bound to the chair, his hands zip tied behind his back. The man craned his neck at an awkward angle, his fearful eyes riveted on Jacob as he approached.

"Don't kill me," he said hoarsely. "I'm a federal agent."

"I'm here to help," Jacob said, assessing the situation. "I'm gonna cut you loose, okay?"

The man nodded.

Using his drop point pocket knife, Jacob rapidly sawed through the plastic ties.

"What's your name?"

"Craig Phillips."

"My name is Jacob. I'll get you out of this."

After freeing Phillips, Jacob peered into the one room cabin. The body of the second man, his hands and legs bound, lay in a pool of frozen blood on the floor, face down.

"He's dead," Phillips whispered.

"Can you stand up?"

"I don't think so."

"Did they shoot you?"

"No, they beat me. One of them stuck me a couple times but they didn't want to kill me. I don't know why. You got water? I haven't had a drink since they left."

Jacob marveled at the agent's composure, opened a bottle of water from his daypack and held it out to him. Phillips tried to grab it but it fell from his hand. Jacob held it to the agent's lips, pulling it away after several gulps.

"No more for now. We need to get outta here."

"They're coming back, aren't they?"

"I don't know. But let's get you into my sled."

Clothed in blue jeans and a bloodied T-shirt, the agent struggled to help Jacob get him to his feet. Movement was difficult. His legs were rubbery and his head ached from the beatings. Jacob could feel the agent's heart beating rapidly as he supported him from behind, his arms wrapped under his shoulders and across his chest. He was shivering uncontrollably as Jacob wrapped a blanket around him before lowering him onto the sled. He placed the pillows under the agent's head and spread another blanket over his body, his knees bent so that he was entirely inside the sled.

There was no shortcut to take with the heavy load as Jacob grabbed the rope and, with great effort, got the sled moving, scanning the area ahead for open ice, which would make for less drag. Even so, he was sweating profusely, overheating despite the cold and falling snow, and he could feel his energy level dropping with every step. It had been a long, exhausting day and by all rights he should have been sipping a brandy in his comfy cabin. But resting wasn't an option, not with the roar of a diesel engine suddenly puncturing the quiet.

"Did you call the police?" the agent asked, his voice weakening.

Jacob ignored the question, not sure what to say, but when he glanced back at the sled, the agent was grimacing and tears were running down his cheeks.

27

Larsen did as Benny told him, slowly zigzagging up the road until he could no longer see County M in the rearview where Wiley Crawford and his thugs waited while watching the big truck push snow into the woods. The plan was to follow the plow in the SUVs. They were anxious, watching for traffic, not knowing how much time they had before another deputy showed up. Ten minutes went by like an eternity as they stood alongside their cars, snow falling steadily, their nerves on edge.

"We should be going," Tony said.

"Not yet," Crawford said.

"What are we waiting for?"

Crawford sighed.

"Wait till the truck is outta sight."

"But why?" he whined.

"So once we get up there, nobody can see the cars," Michael Gerlach said, irritated. "Ain't that right, major?"

"That's right, sergeant. Worst thing would be for the cops to come by while we're driving into the woods."

"You don't think they'll see the road's been plowed?"

"Not if they're driving by. They'll be looking for their buddy, not us."

"I don't like it," Tony Mumphrey griped. "We shoulda never gone into town in the first place."

"It's too late for that, private," Crawford said stiffly. "Besides, we'd be snowed in anyway."

"And we wouldn't have a plow to dig us out," Gerlach agreed.

Tony shook his head and moved toward the center of the road, staring into the woods as the plow disappeared from view. He was looking for a way to mitigate his blunder for having killed the deputy. He'd completely misread the situation and it was important not to be seen as the cause of their predicament. Pointing at the logging road, he returned to the cars.

"There, see, can't see it anymore. Can we go now?"

"Don't be such a whiner," Gerlach said, harshly.

28

REACHING THE TOP OF A RIDGE, THE LOGGING ROAD
straightened enough that Eric Larsen had a clear view of his
surroundings. The forest had been cut back from the road,
leaving wide but steep snow-covered aprons on either side.
Static crackled on Benny's two-way radio.

"Yeah," he said, holding the device in front of his face
like a microphone.

"Stop for a minute," Crawford said, as his SUV topped
the hill.

Larsen took the truck out of gear. He watched as the
cars crowded behind him. Gerlach approached the
passenger side, rapping on the door, stepping back as it
swung open.

"Hey, little guy," Benny said jovially, looking down at
the sergeant.

"Careful, you almost hit me with the door. Wiley wants
to talk."

Benny looked at the driver.

"What about him?"

"What about him?"

"He might drive off."

"Yeah, at what, five miles an hour?"

Larsen kept his hands on the wheel, his eyes glued to the windshield, the wipers slapping rhythmically at the snow. While they retreated to the lead car, his first thought was that they were right. No way he could build up enough speed quickly enough to make a break. And the snow was too deep to run for it. But what would they do if he tried? If they killed him, they'd be stuck. The only thing they could do was to back down the road, a difficult task. It wouldn't take much to drive off the edge and down a slope or into a ditch.

They could beat him, but that seemed a small price to pay for a chance at freedom. Of course, one of them could lose control and shoot him. He could lock the doors and take his chances but it occurred to him that all they needed to do was break a window. But even if they did, would they shoot him?

What if, when Benny returned, Larsen did what he'd thought about doing earlier? He was bigger and stronger. One well placed blow across the throat was all it would take to incapacitate Benny. And then he'd have a gun, maybe. And his companions wouldn't even know it. He could drive as fast as the snow would allow and if it came to that he could steer the behemoth down a slope and take his chances with gravity.

No, that wouldn't work. The truck would be wrecked and if he survived, they'd kill him for sure. If only he could get a handle on his options. Settle on a plan and then let the chips fall. Somehow he had to get up enough nerve to do something crazy. Something he would never have thought himself capable of doing given that the only certainty was that when they arrived at their destination they would no longer need him. And as much as he didn't want to think about it, he would be dead.

29

Larsen locked the doors as Benny returned to the truck. Putting the transmission in gear, he slowly let up on the clutch, the massive vehicle creeping forward while Benny hoisted himself onto the icy running board, one hand on a grab bar, the other on the door handle.

"What the fuck? Open the door," he shouted, squeezing the grab bar while reaching for his pistol, nearly losing his footing in the process.

It wasn't much of an escape plan as Larsen quickly took the vehicle out of gear and reached over to unlock the passenger door.

"Sorry," he said. "I always lock the door. It's just a habit."

"Thought you could drive away, huh?"

"Yeah, right. At two miles an hour."

"That's bullshit. I know what you was trying to do," Benny said, pointing his pistol as the door swung open of its own accord.

"You gotta shut it hard."

Benny struggled to get his hand on the door while

keeping the pistol on the driver. Gerlach sprang out of the first car, moving quickly to the truck.

"What the fuck is going on, corporal?" he demanded, looking up at Benny, who stood awkwardly on one leg, his arm stretched as far as he could to get a hand on the door.

"He tried to drive off," he said breathlessly. "Gimme a hand, will ya?"

Gerlach rolled his eyes, pushed Benny onto the passenger seat and swung the door so that Benny could reach it easily.

"Just a minute. Let me talk to Wiley," the sergeant said, returning after a brief conversation to the driver's side door. He motioned for Larsen to roll down the window. He held Larsen's phone so that the driver could see the device's wallpaper, a photo of a woman and young girl.

"Just so you know, we know where you live. Think about that next time you try something stupid. Or do I have to draw you a picture?"

———————

It took several minutes before Larsen was no longer seeing red. It was all he could do to keep from launching himself at Benny and twisting his skinny neck. His chest pounded, he was lightheaded and for a moment he thought he was about to have a heart attack. But he settled down quickly realizing that anger wouldn't solve his problem. He needed to clear his head, focus, think through the threat to his family. Normally not a talkative man, he was a good listener. Content until this point to simply do what they instructed, he changed his tactics. He needed information. If he was going to survive, he needed to learn where they were headed so that he'd know where the end of the line was before they got there.

Unlike Larsen, Benny talked incessantly and what he liked to talk about most was himself. The driver picked up on this almost from the start but until now hadn't paid him much attention, focusing instead on the plowing while trying to decide what he would do when the time came. At one point, Eric asked about the man he called major.

"He's our boss."

"Is that his name? Major?"

"That's his rank."

"What's your rank?"

"Right now, I'm a corporal. But one day I'll move up."

"How about the other guys?"

"Mikey is a sergeant and Tony is a private. He's a new guy and kinda on probation right now but after this I don't know what'll happen to him. He blew a cop away and it really pissed off the major. I never seen him so mad."

Larsen nearly ran into a tree after hearing this. He was at a loss for words. He could very well have known the dead officer. A small county didn't have a lot of employees and many wore several hats. When Larsen wasn't driving trucks, he worked in the maintenance shed. It wasn't quite like a family operation, but it was close.

"You some kind of gang?"

"We're an organization. People call us all sorts of things, but they don't know."

"Like a political party?"

"No, bro," Benny said. "We're way more than that. We're about giving power to people like you and me, you know, white people, God's people."

"You religious?"

"You better believe it. When Jesus comes back he's

gonna kick ass. He ain't gonna turn the other cheek, that's for sure."

"You know, Jesus was a Jew."

"Bullshit, was not," Benny said heatedly. "That's what the Jews want you to think. They killed him. He's white just like us and he's buff, man. Lifts weights getting ready for the end times."

Eric wanted to tell Benny that he was delusional but at the same time he didn't want to interrupt his captor's train of thought. The last thing he wanted to do was to get into an argument. What he needed to do was to let him talk, let him get distracted by his own thoughts, put him off his guard.

"You know, come to think of it, you might wanna join us. We could use a guy like you," Benny said.

"I don't know. I don't even know what it is you do."

"Right now the major says we gotta commit crimes to fund the organization."

"Is he the top guy?"

"There's colonels and generals. It's like an army."

"That why you wear camo?"

"Far as I know. We get training and lectures and shit but I was never good in school. Didn't actually graduate. But that don't matter with the organization. The most important stuff is what I already know."

"What do you call yourselves?"

"Patriots, bro. Can't you tell? We're here to put things right, to make things the way they useta be when white people ran the country and we didn't have to put up with fucking minorities and Jew lawyers."

"I mean, your organization."

"Oh. We're the Sovereign Resistance Army. But we're not the only one. There's a lot of us out there all over the country getting ready for the big day when we take over.

But, you know, being a corporal, they don't tell me everything. And I'm fine with that. I'm a soldier. That's good enough for me."

Making slow progress, the plow blade hit something in the road that caused the truck to shudder and stop in its tracks, lifting the front wheels off the ground.

"What was that?" Benny exclaimed.

"I think we hit a rock. Gotta raise the blade a bit. That's the trouble with these back roads, especially in the winter."

"Good thing we were going slow, huh?"

"Definitely. Big as this truck is, it ain't indestructible."

Larsen could see the cars in the side mirror. They stopped as soon as the truck stopped. Nobody got out to investigate. They were far enough behind that if he bashed his passenger's head against the dashboard and took his gun, he might be able to escape without leaving the truck. But he didn't know where they were going. Benny gave him directions only as he needed them. When he asked where they were headed, Benny grinned.

"I know what you're thinking, bro. Just drive like I tell you. Won't be much longer."

WHEN THE GOING GETS TOUGH, THE TOUGH GET GOING, Jacob told himself as he tugged on the rope, putting all his weight into it, pulling the sled through the impossible snow. The curved front of the sled plowed under the light, deep snow with every step, forcing him to clear the buildup frequently. Several times, leaning into the rope with his entire two hundred fifteen pounds, he laid out his five-ten frame as if preparing to dive. If only the snow was packed so that the sled would have something solid beneath it. It was like trying to navigate through a mountain of sawdust.

Sweating profusely even with his coat unzipped, his breathing labored, he made his way up the long incline that led to the ridgeline that led to his cabin. But even when he made the ridge, the going remained difficult as the sled continued to sink in the new snow. Serving as a reminder of the larger situation was the sound of what he determined was a plow on the other side of the valley. The engine noise came and went but he was certain it was a big diesel. What could it be besides a plow? He thought he saw wisps of black exhaust somewhere in the trees. There was little doubt where the machine was headed. He wondered whether it was the police or the killers. How would the cop killers get hold of a snowplow?

Consumed by the sheer physicality of his task, he didn't want to waste the time it would have taken to wave his cell phone to find a signal. Taking a break might erode his resolve, his body surrendering to his fatigue. There was no doubt in his mind that this was the most difficult physical feat he'd undertaken since high school, and his body let him know it. Even though he wasn't running, he had to stop to catch his breath. He wondered if the breathlessness was what his old man experienced from his COPD. Once or twice he stopped, bent over, his hands on his knees, his chest heaving like a bellows, terror welling in his eyes as the next breath seemed out of reach, finally, forcing himself to take short, rapid breaths on the verge of hyperventilating as oxygen finally reached his lungs.

If only his cargo would wake up and help him out. He lay there in the black tub, his legs pulled up, blankets tucked in, dead weight. Perhaps, once at the cabin, the man would wake and explain what had happened. Maybe he wasn't asleep. Maybe he was faking it. Every now and then Jacob would say something aloud, as if to the unconscious man but meant for his own ears, to feed his own psyche. Phrases to keep him motivated, to keep him from giving in to his weariness.

"We're almost there, buddy."

LARSEN KNEW THE END WAS NEAR. HE HAD A CLEAR

view of the snow-covered road, the rising hillside to his left, descending to a frozen pond on the right side. It wouldn't take much to send the truck down the hill, studded with pine, cedar and spruce. If he played his cards right, he could take a sharp angle and maybe reach the bottom upright, which he estimated was forty feet below the road. The worst that could happen would be if the front wheels caught a stump or rock, twisting the steering wheel out of his hands, the behemoth's twenty-five tons rolling over sideways out of control. He had to do what he could do to survive. It was the only way he could be sure his family was safe.

Would they go after his family if he was dead? Why would they? he thought. But what good would he be to his wife and their daughter? He was certain he couldn't talk himself out of the situation. They'd killed a cop. There was no reason to spare him.

"It's not far now," Benny said enthusiastically, pointing out the window with his handgun.

Larsen leaned over to get a better view. Barely visible was a line of several small cabins at the bottom of the slope.

"So, which one you going to?"

"The far one."

Looking out his side mirror, Larsen saw that the cars had yet to make the final turn, the drivers preferring not to fight the clouds of snow thrown up as the truck bulled its way through the snow. Another hundred yards and it would be over. How much time did he have left? Five minutes? It was the longest straight stretch since he'd left the county road. As much as he loved his family, he also loved life. And as long as he was alive, he'd protect them. There was no choice.

"You know what they called me in high school?" he said as Benny looked out the window.

"What?"

"Eric the Red. I'm a fucking Viking."

31

JACOB NEARLY LOST CONTROL OF THE SLED AS HE struggled to ease it from the ridge to his cabin below, a descent of about fifteen feet. Not as much snow reached the ground here and most of what was there was icy and compacted from use. Tying the rope around his waist, he let the sled gently slip onto the path where it immediately pulled on him like a ton of bricks. As hard as it was to pull the sled through the snow, it was just as difficult to keep the sled from breaking away and either crashing into the cabin or rocketing past it and launching itself into the air and crashing into the frozen pond below. Panic seized him as he braced himself against a tree, stopping the sled in its tracks and allowing him to lower it step by step until he reached level ground and the back door.

"Goddamn, I did it," he said triumphantly, as he looked at his silent companion, realizing that the ordeal wasn't over yet.

"We gotta get you inside," he told the man as he stepped inside his cabin. "We gotta get you fixed up."

"I think I can get up," Phillips said hoarsely.

"You're awake."

"I've been in and out of it. What time is it?"

"About four. It's starting to get dark. Can you get up?"

"I think so."

"Here, let's get these blankets off you first," Jacob said.

The top blanket came off easily. The second blanket was bloody. He could see immediately that several of the agent's fingers were broken and that his arms were covered with burn marks and small punctures.

"How do I look?" Phillips asked, grimacing.

"Like shit. But at least you're alive. Let's get you inside."

32

Jacob worked quickly once he'd helped his companion into a chair. He gave him water in a glass and a handful of snack bars and then realized that the agent couldn't grab them with his broken hands.

"If you can put it between my little finger and palm, I think I can hold the bars," he said. "I can't hold the glass."

Jacob held the glass, followed by another, while the man drank noisily.

Finishing his drink, the agent ate several snack bars while Jacob rummaged through his medicine cabinet. Though he tried to hide it, Phillips was in obvious pain.

"I got these from the dentist years ago. They're pain killers. Don't know if they're any good, but they might help."

Phillips glanced at the bottle. Vicodin. The dosage was no longer visible on the label. He nodded. Jacob opened the bottle and put one of the white pills on Phillips' tongue.

"It might help," he said, and asked for more water.

Jacob helped Phillips out of his bloody clothing and into a pair of sweatpants and flannel shirt. The cabin was cold and the agent was shivering, even after putting on the dry clothing.

"Can you turn on the heat?"

"Let me check something first," Jacob said as he went out the front door with his binoculars. It was late afternoon, the sky was gray and the light was fading. The killers had not returned but the snowplow was much closer, the telltale knocking of the diesel engine growing louder.

"What's up?" Phillips asked when Jacob returned.

"There's a snowplow on the other side. It's getting close."

"Is it them?"

"I don't know. You okay?"

"Yeah. Cold."

Phillips watched as Jacob pulled a comforter off his bed, draping it gingerly over the agent's shoulders, tucking it in behind his back as he leaned forward, and wrapping it around his legs.

"This should help. But if I start a fire they'll know we're here. Don't want to do that until we know who it is."

"I understand."

Retrieving his rifle from the sled, Jacob laid it across the table along with his handgun and magazines.

"That's all you got?"

"Yeah."

"They got ARs and an RPG that I know of."

"Let's hope it's the cops coming up the road. I called 911 and they sent out a sheriff's deputy."

"Well, that's good."

"Yeah, except the fuckers killed him."

33

SLUMPING INTO A CHAIR ACROSS THE TABLE FROM Phillips, Jacob's exhaustion finally caught up with him. Feeling much older than his fifty-three years, he wanted nothing more than to take a nap but he knew if he fell asleep it would be hard to wake up. Although his joints and muscles ached, the pain in his right shoulder was worse. He'd injured it playing football and it had never healed properly. It was a low-grade ache that came and went of its own accord.

"How's that pill working for you?"

"I think it's helping."

Jacob thought about taking one himself, for his shoulder. But he knew it would make him feel euphoric, which would not be helpful in his situation. As much as he wanted just to lie back and forget about the world, he knew he couldn't. He needed to be alert, to be decisive. So he made a pot of coffee, which he shared with Phillips, who had to lower his mouth to the cup as he steadied it between his fragile hands. For a moment, sipping the acidic brew, the cabin filled with the smoky aroma of fresh coffee, Jacob leaned back against his chair and slowly exhaled, having given himself permission to relax. It seemed normal. Two guys at a table drinking coffee.

"What happened over there?" Jacob asked.

Phillips sighed.

"It was an undercover operation. I was working with an informant, gathering intel on this gang, but it wasn't supposed to go down the way it did."

"What kind of gang?"

"A mash-up of sovereign citizens and Christian Identity, which is an oxymoron if I ever heard one," Phillips said. "This particular group calls itself the Sovereign Resistance. What they really are is a gang of urban terrorists who commit crimes to fund their lifestyle."

"What about the other guy?"

"He was my informant. At some point, he found Jesus, the one in the Bible. He said he needed to atone for what he'd done. Used the word *atone*. Needed to, you know. He said Jesus told him he needed to do it. It was like out of his hands. He told me this over and over like he was trying to remind himself that he wasn't acting of his own volition."

"They wanted to kill him because he found Jesus?"

"He quit the organization and they had second thoughts about it, from what I could gather. I didn't get the impression he was gonna turn on them but for some reason they wanted him dead. I mean he was just a twenty-something kid who was trying to get his head on straight," Phillips said bitterly.

"Weird."

"Yeah, but I gotta hand it to him, it took balls. He was amazing, actually."

"Amazing, huh?"

"You look at me and you think I got the worst of it, but

what they did to me was nothing compared to what they did to him. And all the while, at least while he was conscious, he kept praying, not fighting, not arguing, just looking at the ceiling. They set me in front of him so I could watch what they did. It was really hard. I had to keep telling myself that I was gathering intel in order to prosecute these guys. When I tried to look away, they'd burn me or stick me with a pen knife."

Jacob wasn't sure whether he wanted to hear more details, though the Vicodin seemed to have loosened Phillips' tongue.

"So, how you feeling?"

"I can't feel my fingers, otherwise, not so bad. I'm liking the Vicodin. I'm grateful for that."

"You tired? Anything I can do to make you more comfortable?"

"I'm fine where I am. I've got things under control. I just don't want to move if I don't have to. Not right now."

"The bleeding looks under control," Jacob said, looking at the dried blood on the agent's forearms.

"They didn't go deep. It looks worse than it is, I'm sure."

Phillips continued to talk about his ordeal, as if to intensify his recollection of what had happened or exorcise it. Tears welled as he described how he had watched his informant die and prepared himself to die but got an unexpected reprieve when his tormentors left for the evening.

Jacob listened distractedly as he moved about the cabin, glancing out the window across the valley, expecting to see a snowplow at any time. He wondered about the accuracy of rocket propelled grenades, as well as their range. How close did they have to be to hit the cabin?

Although he was curious, Jacob didn't press the agent for details about the torture.

"Why didn't they kill you?" Jacob asked after Phillips had finished talking.

"I have no idea. Maybe they were thrown off by how Glen held up. He told them he was a martyr for Christ and that whatever they did to him was less than Jesus had suffered. He was remarkable, really. I think he died before they were finished and that's when they started pounding me until I lost consciousness. For whatever reason, they left me there. That's why I knew they were coming back."

"So, when you regained consciousness, you were thinking they were going to kill you?"

"At that point all I was thinking about was escaping. If it weren't for you, I'd still be down there, maybe stretched out on the ice. But I would have been crawling like that right up to the point they put a bullet in my brain."

Jacob smiled admiringly and briefly wondered what he would do in a similar situation. And then he realized how much of a chance he'd taken to rescue the agent, knowing that if the killers had appeared while they were in the open, he would have stood little chance of defending himself. Instead of one dead agent, there would be one dead agent and one dead borderline hermit.

But his self-reflection was cut short as headlights appeared on the other side of the valley. It was going on five o'clock, the woods were darkening, snow had stopped falling and the overcast sky was clearing. It was going to get cold. He put on his parka, grabbed the deer rifle, pistol and binoculars and hurried to the back door.

"What's up?" Phillips asked.

"They're here. I'm gonna check things out."

"Don't let them see you," the agent said earnestly.

"Don't worry. I won't."

34

BENNY WASN'T CERTAIN WHAT TO MAKE OF THE DRIVER when he shouted something about being a Viking.

"What the fuck?" was as far as he got when Eric the Red turned sharply to the right, directing the big diesel off the road, the front end suddenly dipping, gathering speed, his hands squeezing the steering wheel. Benny hit the ceiling as the truck seemed to drop out from under him. Then he slammed head first against the dashboard, his body sliding limply onto the expansive floor.

Larsen fought against the urge to stand on the brake pedal, even as the truck bounced onto the ice like a child's toy, the ice cracking into countless fractures, the vehicle slowly pirouetting until it crashed nose first into the hillside below Jacob's cabin, its engine dying as a cloud of steam erupted from under the hood. The driver remained frozen for a moment, his hands shaking uncontrollably as he released his shoulder harness. His captor lay crumpled on the floor, unmoving, his pistol nowhere in sight. Even though he feared the others would be after him, Larsen stretched across the seat, reaching under Benny's body, feeling for the gun. No such luck. Anxiety infected him like a virus. He needed to give up on the gun and make a run for it. He could see their headlights on the opposite side but nothing more. Unlocking the driver's side door, he kicked it open, his hand wrapped around a grab bar, ready to swing onto the running board when several bullets slammed into the door panel, followed by several more through the rear window and out the windshield.

He wanted desperately to see what was going on, where they were, but was afraid to expose himself. The only thing he could do was to find the gun, be ready when they got close, hoping he'd have half a chance. But lying low on the seat, he didn't have the kind of leverage required to push Benny out of the way. He couldn't tell if Benny was breathing and didn't care. All he wanted was the gun.

"Where is it, goddamn it?" he mumbled, frustrated.

Kicking open the passenger door, he pushed Benny out, his head landing on the running board, his legs bent at the knees across the lower door frame. No luck. He felt for the gun under the seat. No luck.

How much longer did he have? He told himself to forget about the gun. He was a sitting duck in the truck. He had no choice. Unarmed, unprotected he had to make a run for it. He tried to remember what he'd seen of the pond. He'd seen a cabin somewhere above him. Was there anything he could hide behind? Would it be better to run to one side or another? What would be harder for them to hit, someone climbing a hill or someone running? If only he could see where they were. There was no point in thinking about it. They would hit him or they wouldn't.

And then he heard the report of something he knew well. A deer rifle.

35

Jacob had just cozied into a position on the edge
of his property overlooking the pond when the snowplow
veered off the road and down the opposite slope. It looked as
if it was moving in slow motion until it reached the ice,
where it seemed to gain speed. Parts flew off of it as it
bounced. Not wanting to expose himself, he couldn't see
where it ended up but he could smell the steaming coolant.
Somehow, the driver had kept it upright on its descent. But
why had he done it? Who drives a snowplow off the road
and down a hill?

That's when he saw the SUVs make the turn and stop
at the point where the plow had left the road, obscured by a
veil of settling snow. He'd been hoping the police were
behind the plow, but now it was clear that the killers had
returned. And then they started shooting. At first, he feared
they were shooting at him but he realized quickly they were
shooting at the truck. That meant whoever was driving
wasn't part of their gang. Although they were firing from an
exposed position, they were shrouded in the forest's darkness. There was daylight in the tops of the trees, but it was

already night at ground level. He couldn't get a clear shot but at the same time felt uneasy about aiming at a human. He sometimes felt that way when he went deer hunting. Not a trophy hunter, he'd sight a majestic twelve-point buck and hesitate, admiring its muscular beauty, the symmetry of its antlers, and then not take the shot, letting it live another day. Would he hesitate to squeeze the trigger when a human was in the crosshairs of his scope? Was he ready for that?

So he fired a round at the lead SUV, putting out its passenger side headlight. That got their attention.

36

Major Wiley Crawford was in the lead vehicle. Tony, the private, the recruit, drove the second car and leaped out of the vehicle as soon as Crawford's car stopped. They had followed well behind the plow to avoid the Niagara of snow the big truck kicked up. It had taken so long to get this far that they'd have to drive through the woods in the dark to get back to the county road. He wondered if there was a quicker way out. The radio they'd taken from the deputy rested on the center console. He'd hoped to use it to listen in on the police, certain that it wouldn't be long before they found their dead deputy. But it broadcast mostly static and the occasional code that he couldn't understand. Trying to be helpful, Tony guessed at what the codes meant.

"Why don't you just shut up about that?" Crawford scolded. "Guessing don't help."

They should have finished the job yesterday. Should have just killed the fed and burned the cabin to the ground and made their getaway to Michigan. But no. He had to listen to Benny's whining about spending the night with a corpse. What harm would it do to spend a night at a hotel? The fed wasn't going anywhere and they'd already taken care of the Jesus freak turncoat. But the major thought the fed had more to say and he knew the guys were upset over how long Glen had lasted and how he just kept praying, talking to Jesus and seemingly not caring about the pain they were inflicting. It would have gone easier for him if he'd simply told them what he'd said to the agent. He could tell his crew was unnerved. They'd been shouting at their victim the whole time, calling him names, laughing as they tortured him only to become withdrawn and silent when it was over. Benny had brought up leaving the cabin. None of the others objected. Not even Crawford, though he believed he could get more intel out of the fed and rationalized the departure by letting himself think that the agent would be more compliant the next day, if he survived the night. He'd expected to get an early start, be back at the cabin in less than an hour, extract what they could from the agent, put out his lights, destroy the evidence, hide the body and be back at the compound before dark. Fucking snow. Fucking fed.

It was while he was embedded in this train of thought that he watched in disbelief as the truck plummeted down the hill just as his car had turned the corner for what should have been the last leg of the journey. Things had just gone from bad to worse.

Michael Gerlach reacted like a soldier, grabbing his AR-15, positioning himself on the hillside amidst the torn up slope, waiting for one or another door to open, firing reflexively when it did. For good measure he sent several rounds through the rear window. That's when the major told him to stop firing.

"You might hit Benny," he said.

"If he ain't dead already," the sergeant said, crouching against a tree.

"You got him pinned down," Crawford said. "Don't shoot unless you see him, okay?"

Gerlach nodded without taking his eyes off the truck.

"It's getting dark," he said. "We won't be able to see him. If we don't do something, he's gonna get away. I say we go down there. He's not armed. What's he gonna do besides run? I'll take him out like a rabbit."

"Get your AR," Crawford said to the rookie, as he stepped out of the SUV.

Just as Tony took a step, the headlamp exploded and the valley resonated with the report of Jacob's deer rifle.

"Holy shit," Tony exclaimed as he scrambled for cover.

37

Jacob regretted taking the shot almost immediately. Several slugs buried themselves in nearby trees as he flattened himself in the snow. He'd never been shot at before. It made his heart skip a beat.

Why had he revealed himself like that? Just minutes ago he'd assured Craig Phillips that he wouldn't expose his position and then he fired a round, producing a muzzle flash and cloud of white smoke that invited a response from the other side. He had given away his position. He had made his cabin a target. And for what? He was grateful that they were on the other side and that it was getting dark. He watched through his binoculars as they made their way, silhouettes among the shadows, to the cabin, entering it through the back door and almost immediately shutting the front door.

Turning his attention to the plow, he repositioned himself for a better view, confident that the killers couldn't shoot at him without leaving the cabin. Cautiously leaning over the ledge, he noticed immediately that it was a county vehicle, that both of its doors were open and that someone was inside. Setting his rifle down, he drew his pistol and tossed a small stone that struck the hood dead center. The person inside pressed his face against the windshield, looking toward Jacob.

"Who are you?"

"Eric Larsen," he shouted. "I work for the county."

"What are you doing here?"

"They forced me to drive."

"Why don't you step out where I can see you?"

"They'll shoot me."

"No, they won't. They're in that cabin down there."

To be on the safe side, Larsen exited via the passenger door, careful to avoid stepping on Benny, who was sprawled across the running board, half in and half out of the cab, emerging with his hands up.

"Can you not point your gun at me? Please."

"Are you armed?"

"No."

Jacob, pistol still in hand, directed Larsen to join him and watched carefully as he ascended the hillside. Confident that he was in control of the situation, he stood, brushed off snow, shouldered his rifle, turning his back on the pond to meet the driver as he reached the top.

"You don't have to worry about me," Larsen said. "I really appreciate your help. I thought they were gonna kill me."

"That why you drove down the hill?"

"Yeah. Do you know what the fuck is going on, mister?"

38

THOUGH HE'D LOST CONSCIOUSNESS AFTER HITTING HIS head, Benny regained it but played dead, having lost his pistol. He'd have shot the driver if he had it, but he was no match in a fight against the larger, stronger Larsen. His mind was running on two tracks at this point. Now that the driver had left, his opportunity to escape had arrived. If only he could find the pistol. He felt around for it, as far as he could reach under the seat, across the dark floor, the dashboard, the seat itself. Nothing. He could hear them talking above. Couldn't make out the words but he didn't want to make his move while they stood there. At the same time, he wondered what his companions would have to say about losing the plow. All they could do now was return the way they had come, ending up on the county road, which by now might be crawling with cops.

How would they get out of this? If only Tony hadn't killed the cop. What was he thinking? Benny could tell that the major had been surprised when it happened and seemed upset about it. But then, they'd killed an informer and had a federal agent tied up in the cabin. It had all gone to hell so quickly. This was not how it was supposed to happen. They hadn't planned on any of it. They were going to extract information. Find out if there were infiltrators. But it was never clear to him what they would do once they had what they were looking for. How could they let the agent live? He hadn't thought it out himself at the time, relying on the major, who seemed to know what he was doing. He focused on his duties and nothing more. The major was in charge of the big picture. All Benny had to do was to follow orders, but he couldn't help but feel that Tony had ruined it by improvising on the cop. They should never have gone back to the cabin after that.

"Hindsight is twenty-twenty," he told himself as he waited until he could no longer hear the men.

39

"I wish you'd said that right off the bat," Jacob quibbled after Larsen told him about Benny.

"I thought he was dead."

"But you don't know?"

"I didn't take his pulse," Larsen said testily. "So, no, I don't know."

They'd been in the cabin for several minutes. Jacob had already removed his parka and was working on starting a fire since he no longer worried whether the smoke could be seen.

"I saw him hit his head a coupla times," Larsen said. "I know he was knocked out. I saw blood but I was more worried about myself. Besides, he had a gun. If he was conscious he'd have shot me."

Jacob grabbed his rifle and dashed out of the cabin, taking a position on the ledge overlooking the truck, sighting through the scope. Had the man fled? There were no obvious signs that Jacob could make out. No footprints to give him away. Was he still in the truck? If so, was he conscious? The fact that he had a gun made it too risky to find out.

"It looks like he's still in the truck," Jacob said after reentering the cabin. "But I'm not going down there to find out."

Larsen nodded in agreement, having taken a seat at the table. Phillips sat up on the bed, listening to the conversation, as Jacob described how his day went. Larsen had his turn and then Phillips filled them in on what he knew about their adversaries, whom he described as domestic terrorists.

"All I know is the guy I was with was kinda nuts," Larsen said.

"My question is what are they gonna do?" Jacob said, anxiously.

"What can they do? It's dark."

"What if they got night-vision goggles?"

"Why would they have that?"

"They got an RPG," Jacob said. "And assault rifles. Ain't that right, Craig?"

Phillips nodded.

"An RPG? Really?"

"I saw it. Didn't see night-vision gear, but I can't say they don't have it."

"So, what's stopping them?"

"Ever fire an RPG?" Phillips asked rhetorically. "Takes practice. They're accurate over short distances but it's easy to miss what you're aiming at. I'm guessing they got only one rocket and they're not going to waste it at night."

"So, we're okay here?" Larsen asked.

"That would be my guess," Phillips said.

"Well, I'm gonna keep an eye on the guy in the truck," Jacob said, as he zipped his parka and stepped out of the cabin with his rifle.

40

"What do we do now, major?" Michael Gerlach, the sergeant, asked.

The three members of the Sovereign Resistance milled about the cabin, lit by the harsh light of a pair of LED lanterns, carefully avoiding the tortured body of turncoat Glen Adams, which was frozen to the floor.

"I'm just glad we can't see his face," Gerlach said. "This place is creeping me out."

"Yeah, we need to get outta here. Pronto," Tony said.

Major Wiley Crawford settled into a chair at the small table, a lantern hanging from a hook overhead. The operation had not gone the way he'd expected. They'd come to Wisconsin to track down Adams, whom they now suspected of collaborating with an FBI agent. He'd been with the group long enough to know its inner workings. He knew the members. He had direct knowledge of their criminal activity. He knew where their money came from. And he was all in with them until he got too religious. Until he started the crazy talk about Jesus and atonement, which went on for weeks before the generals decided he was affecting morale.

They gave him an ultimatum—keep the preaching to himself or leave.

At first they were relieved that he left. They'd gotten rid of a nut job before he could do any real damage. And then the misgivings flooded in, like late arriving ballots in a contested election. Although he didn't know where all the bodies were buried, he knew enough to put all of them in prison for life. No one who had ever been initiated into the organization had quit before and that may have been why their reassessment was late arriving. All they wanted to do was pull the painful tooth, and only after they'd done so and the pain was relieved did they feel a gap where the tooth used to be and realized they had a new problem to solve.

There was no animosity at the parting. He'd told them he was returning to his home town of Hayward, Wisconsin, where he planned to conduct a ministry. They helped him pack, gave him bus fare and enough cash to get by for several months. They'd welcome him back if he changed his mind and his religious fervor, but they could tell by the knowing smile that they would never see him again.

"If it wasn't for that rat bastard lying there, we wouldn't be in this jam," Tony said, standing over the body, resisting an urge to kick it.

"Bullshit," Crawford said angrily. "I shouldn't have listened to Benny. Driving into town like that. Staying in a motel."

"If we stayed, we'd be snowed in. Just look at what it took to get up here."

"Yeah, and now we got a fucking federal agent on the loose. How the fuck did he get away?"

"I know where he is," Gerlach said.

"You mean up in that cabin," Crawford said matter-of-factly.

"Yeah. He couldn'ta got away on his own."

"Who the fuck cares? It won't be long before the cops are crawling all over the place. We're sitting ducks here," Tony said, standing alongside Crawford, who suddenly slammed his fist on the table, rising, his face close to Tony's.

"If it hadn't been for you killing that cop, maybe we wouldn't be in this situation. Nobody gave you instructions to do that. You didn't hear me issue an order, did you?"

Tony lowered his head slightly while Gerlach eyed the two warily. He wondered whether the major was letting off steam or preparing to act out.

"Stop arguing," Gerlach pleaded, "We need to focus on a plan."

41

SPECIAL AGENT CRAIG PHILLIPS, WHO WAS IN DETROIT to meet with supervisors, was dumbfounded when he was told to report to the bus station on Howard Street, that one of the Sovereigns was going somewhere. It wasn't until he'd gotten there, dressed casually in blue jeans and a gray sweatshirt and parka, and carrying a daypack, that he saw Glen Adams for the first time in the flesh. There were plenty of photos of him so he recognized him immediately. Clean shaven, rangy, his tattoos hidden under a flannel shirt and camo pants, he sat in the waiting room, his coat draped across the chair for cushioning, his feet propped on a large, hardshell suitcase. The young man smiled as Phillips took a seat next to him.

"So, where you headed?" Phillips asked after settling in.

"Wisconsin," Adams said.

"Me, too," Phillips said. "You got your ticket?"

"Certainly do," Adams said, pointing to his shirt pocket.

"So you're going to Milwaukee, huh?"

"Actually, I'm headed to Hayward."

"Hayward, huh?"

"It's way up north."

Lying had become second nature to Phillips. It came with the undercover territory. The groups he spied on were suspicious by nature and while he never become a member, he played around the periphery, frequenting bars and other places where his targets gravitated, gathering intel. So far, everything he'd said to Adams was a lie. Now that he knew the young man's destination, he needed a ticket. After five minutes of chitchat, he left for the ticket counter. He knew he could board the bus without a ticket simply by showing his credentials, but he was concerned that showing his badge would invite unwanted attention from other passengers.

"Is there a bus that goes to Hayward, in Wisconsin?" Phillips asked at the counter.

The clerk did some keyboarding.

"No, sir, I can't find one."

"Is there anything close?"

"There's another line you can catch in Milwaukee," the clerk said, peering into his screen. "It looks like Chippewa Falls is the closest."

Phillips thanked the clerk and returned to his seat with his ticket to Milwaukee.

"So, did you get a ticket to Hayward?"

"They don't have a stop in Hayward. I'll prolly get a ticket to Chippewa Falls. That's the closest place."

"Hey, that's where I'm going."

"Really? You got family there?"

Phillips smiled wanly. His mind raced. These were the kinds of off-handed questions that tripped up even the most experienced agents. He'd never been to Chippewa Falls, didn't know the city or its economy. What he did have was training, experience and a talent for lying his way out of awkward situations by concocting plausible explanations on the spur of the moment.

"I've got a job interview."

"Where at?"

"The school district. I'm a teacher."

"That's great," Adams said approvingly. "I'm kind of a teacher myself."

"Is that right?"

"Yessir, I'm a teacher of the Lord's word."

42

JACOB WATCHED AS A MAN SCURRIED ACROSS THE POND like a rabbit. It was too dark to make out details as he sighted the figure in his scope but refrained from squeezing the trigger. He couldn't bring himself to shoot someone in the back, even someone who might not have similar qualms should their situation be reversed. He lost sight of the target as he blended into the darkened woods on the opposite hillside.

"You shoulda taken the shot," Larsen said when Jacob returned to the cabin. "He's the guy had a gun on me. I'd've taken the shot."

"Yeah, well, you should've been out there," Jacob said dismissively. "Anyway, I wasn't looking for him. Far as I can tell, they haven't come out. And the snow's starting to fall again. The sky ain't clearing up like I thought."

It didn't take long for the wood stove to spread its heat and glow, augmenting the wall-mounted LED strips. Phillips lay on the bed, grimacing, his pain returning. Jacob offered another Vicodin.

"Better not," the agent said, waving him off. "I want to have my wits about me if they try something."

Phillips couldn't hide the fact that he was having trouble breathing as he alternated between a series of quick gasps followed by several deep breaths as if he were running out of oxygen. Jacob wondered if the agent had a punctured lung and, if he did, whether there was something he could do to help him. Having had pneumonia, he knew what it was like to struggle to breathe, the incipient panic, the desperation. Larsen also noticed.

"Is he okay?" Larsen whispered.

"No, he's not. They tortured him. Maybe they broke a rib."

Larsen frowned.

"That's not good. Is there anything we can do?"

"Not unless you're an EMT."

"Well, that ain't me."

"But I was thinking, maybe we should take turns watching their cabin."

"You think they're gonna try something?"

"I don't know. I'm worried about the RPG."

43

PHILLIPS WAS CAREFUL NOT TO PUMP ADAMS TOO hard, adopting the persona of a talkative seat mate. The young man was nothing like what the agent expected from a member of the Sovereign Resistance, a criminal enterprise whose ultimate goal seemed to be the overthrow of elected government mixed with elements of racial war and apocalyptic Christianity for good measure. He knew that Adams had lived in the organization's compound, which to him meant he was hard core. Member profiles the agency compiled revealed that the majority lived on their own, had families, held jobs and participated in gang activities mostly on weekends, though most surveillance was focused on the compound.

It should have taken eight hours for the bus to arrive at the Milwaukee Intermodal Station, but icy conditions and traffic stoppages brought them into the city nearly two hours late. Both men purchased tickets for the six-hour ride to Chippewa Falls and, after grazing on vending machine food, settled in for the night in the chilly waiting room. Both men slept fitfully, having dozed intermittently during the ride from Detroit. Adams stepped outside into the cold several times for a cigarette. Phillips woke as the first rays of sunshine pierced the glass building. Clusters of people began infiltrating the station, waiting to board trains and buses as he stumbled out of his chair, his joints stiff and aching. Stretching like a jogger, he shook out his legs and made his way to a bank of vending machines. Someone had placed an upside down paper cup in the coffee machine. There had been times when he couldn't start the day with a cup of coffee, mostly while on the job. But it was not something he would do voluntarily. He'd been starting his day with coffee since he was twelve and, whether it was physical or psychological dependence, he always felt better after a cup of joe. With the single-mindedness of an addict, and the aid of an app on his phone, he located a cafe across the street that opened at five-thirty where he had an Americano and a danish.

Adams was awakening when Phillips returned, nearly two hours before their bus was scheduled to leave. The young man looked disheveled, his long hair sticking out haphazardly, his clothing wrinkled. Phillips realized that he probably looked rumpled as well and brushed his brown hair back with his hand.

"What time is it?" Adams asked sleepily.

"A little after six. How you doing?"

The young man suddenly stood, stretching his arms like a scarecrow, tilting his head back, tilting his neck, shaking out his joints.

"What a great day to be alive," he said, smiling.

And just like that, he bowed his head and prayed, his lips moving in silence. It took only seconds.

"I like to start the day by thanking the Lord. And now I need a smoke."

Phillips nodded.

"You hungry?"

"Man, I am. I could eat a horse."

"How about coffee and a croissant?"

"Yeah, I'd like that. They got croissants here?"

"Across the street. There's a coffeehouse. My treat."

44

THE GENERALS HAD LET HIM LEAVE BECAUSE, AT THE time, it seemed like an easy way to get rid of a problem. But not twelve hours after Adams left the compound did the generals have second thoughts. Distrust was never far from the surface. Their apocalyptic brand of Christianity didn't know what to do with Adams's New Testament evangelism. However, now that he was no longer a member, there was no reason to give him the benefit of the doubt. People were either with them or against them. There was no middle ground. He had become a liability.

"We can't control him," one of them said during a meeting.

"He knows a lot about us."

"He doesn't know everything."

"He knows we got an RPG. Right there that would give the law probable cause to invade the compound."

"Too much religion isn't a good thing," another said. "We let him stay and he's gonna keep preaching and confessing. You can count on it. I've seen this in AA meetings. Some people just can't help themselves, and he's one of them."

As they uncovered one reason after another why Adams posed a threat, it became clear what had to be done. That's when they summoned Major Crawford. It was during the evening on the day that Adams had left.

"It's better this way," one of the generals said. "It might've been a problem if we killed him here. The guys in the ranks liked him. But we know where he's going, right?"

"Burt drove him to Detroit and he told him he's going back to where he grew up. Some small town in Wisconsin. I'll get the name," Crawford said.

"This is gonna work out," one of the three generals said. "Everybody thinks he's gone off to start a new life. Nobody's gonna know but us what happened to him."

"Not if they can't find his body," Crawford said.

45

When he wasn't listening to Adams's plans for the future, his dream of starting a church in the woods, his optimism, Craig Phillips came up with a plan. He didn't want to part with Adams in Chippewa Falls, not when his final destination was a hundred miles to the north in Hayward. He felt the two had hit it off and that with a little more time he could convince the young man to talk about the Sovereigns and how it would help with his atonement, a word the young man had used many times.

Since they couldn't take a bus to Hayward, that left rental cars. From the bus station in Chippewa Falls, they took a cab to the Chippewa Valley Regional Airport, in Eau Claire, where they rented a Ford Fusion.

"It's like I been saying," Adams said as they rolled onto U.S. Highway 53 for the ninety-minute drive to Hayward.

"What's that?"

"The Lord provides."

"I don't understand."

"Do you think it was a coincidence that we were brought together?"

Phillips' instinct was to roll his eyes. Instead, he hesitated like a schoolboy who knew the answer to a question and then, when he was called upon, lost track of it.

"You're not a believer, are you?" Adams asked.

"Not like you."

"Well, you're just not ready. That's okay. No one can make you believe. It's something that you do on your own. Or it just happens."

"Well, you know, it's great that you found God."

"Oh, I didn't find God," Adams said earnestly. "God found me. I was like you, a nonbeliever. Actually, I never even thought about it. I wasn't raised in a religious household. The patriarch of the family was a mean spirit."

Phillips listened attentively as his passenger talked about his life, reviewing it retrospectively as if talking about someone else, how he'd drifted after dropping out of high school, falling into a life of petty crime before turning eighteen. Working undercover for more than a year, the agent was familiar with the hard luck stories he'd heard on the street. Mostly, they were either justifying their actions or pointing out excuses, how they didn't have choices, how they did what they did to survive, even though for some it started out as a pursuit for kicks, or they just wanted to see what they could get away with. Halfway into the drive Phillips realized Adams wasn't excusing his actions but confessing. Nothing that he mentioned amounted to more than a misdemeanor, until he became involved with the Sovereign Resistance, which he admitted freely.

"I still haven't figured out whether I joined or they just adopted me," he said wistfully. "You know, when you're hungry and sleeping in alleys and somebody offers a hand, you take it? At least if you're not mental. I mean, I was down and out. I knew it, too. And I was scared as a cat in a room full of coyotes. I wouldn't admit that to nobody before I found the Savior. I mean, that was one of the things with the Sovereigns—that's what they called themselves, not the army like you'd think but the Sovereigns like it was some kind of title—they hate weakness. They'd pick on you like in junior high if you showed fear. They'd test you, too. I picked up on this right away, so I just told myself whatever happens, happens and even if they put a knife on my throat I wouldn't let them see fear. That wasn't really hard for me, 'cause I was fakin' it my whole life."

"What kinda stuff did you do with these Sovereigns?"

Adams grew pensive, eyeballed the trees as they sped down the highway, their branches covered with snow-like petticoats. Phillips wondered whether he'd pressed too hard.

"You don't have to say anything," the agent said quickly, his eyes fixed on the road. "It just seemed like you—"

"Yeah, it's a part of my life and I need to own it," Adams insisted. "But I'm not proud of it. I'm just glad it was only for a coupla years, and really, I never did buy into their shit, you know, that they're above the government and have rights that no one else has. And I never had anything against blacks or Mexicans. Like I said, they reached out to me when I needed help and maybe if they hadn't I wouldn't have found the Lord, and I'm grateful for that. Like they say, the Lord works in mysterious ways."

46

WILEY CRAWFORD WAS READY TO GIVE CHASE following his meeting with the generals. He loved to get on the road in the black Tahoes with the darkened windows and raised bodies, bereft of insignia, mystery surrounding them as they traveled through the night, one behind the other, on a mission to undo a mistake. The order was simple: solve the problem. As ominous as it sounded, during the drive Crawford was well aware that his quarry didn't know that he was being pursued and wouldn't know it until they had him in custody. It didn't bother him that Adams had gone soft after presenting himself as a willing recruit. He wasn't beefy and angry like most of the others. He was a homeless guy who probably shouldn't have been recruited in the first place. He didn't see him as a threat to the organization the way the generals had come to see him. He thought they were paranoid. He wasn't the first person to wash out, though most of the iffy ones were gone in the first week or two. But he couldn't think of anyone who'd left after being involved for more than a few months, much less two years.

But that didn't prevent them from bringing an arsenal with them. The men in the cars were committed Sovereigns. They lived in the compound, wore their uniform patches proudly and wouldn't shy away from a fight. They knew all the stories about Sovereigns who'd died in firefights with police, martyrs to the cause. They communicated with like-minded groups on the internet using Virtual Private Networks and encryption. They used burn phones. They filed off serial numbers on their weapons, used cash or stolen credit cards for transactions and carried fake IDs.

What was on Crawford's mind as they entered Wisconsin was how they would convince Adams to cooperate. They needed to get him in the car without creating a scene. Then they could find a place in the woods where they could finish him off. Make it look like natural causes, like falling off a cliff. Tony, who rode shotgun, wasn't helpful. Recruited straight out of prison, where he'd belonged to a white power gang, he'd been with the Sovereigns for six months, had gone through the training and indoctrination and was excited about his first assignment.

"That's a hard one, major," he said. "To me, he's a turncoat. Nothing more. You execute turncoats, right?"

The major nodded.

"Pretty clear to me, man. I mean, sir."

When they started the mission, Tony was certain he'd be promoted when it was over, if he did what he was supposed to, which, from the way the generals talked, was to be aggressive.

Crawford wished it had been clear to him. But it wasn't. Adams hadn't done anything against the group. He'd been regarded as a dependable soldier until he got religion. But the generals had a change of mind. It would've been so much better had they not let him leave the compound, shackled him if necessary, and then determined what to do with him.

"I got a question," Tony asked.

"Shoot."

"Why we carrying an RPG and all the ammo?"

"In case we get into a shootout with the cops."

Tony sniffed.

"What?" Crawford asked sharply.

"So this is real, huh? I mean, we could get killed."

Crawford nodded.

47

FROM U.S. HIGHWAY 53, PHILLIPS TURNED ONTO U.S. Highway 63 for the final leg into the small town. Adams's face was pressed against the passenger window as he watched familiar landmarks pass by.

"I'd like to go out to the old place," Adams said. "If you don't mind."

"Where is it?"

Following Adams's directions, they drove past the Freshwater Fishing Hall of Fame and onto County Road B, then took a right on County K, a two-lane asphalt strip cutting through a thick forest.

"Here, here, turn here," Adams said as they passed an unimproved road leading into the woods. Phillips braked, backed up and proceeded slowly into the foot deep snow until Adams waved his hands.

"Here, stop here," he said, leaping out the door just as the car stopped. Phillips watched as Adams pushed through the snow, stopping suddenly in front of an open area surrounded by elm, ash and pine. Several large, blackened timbers jutted out of the snow.

"It's not here anymore," he said disappointedly after returning to the car, staring at the scene in disbelief. "Must've burned down."

"What's not here?"

"Our house. That's where I grew up. It's gone now," he said morosely.

"When was the last time you were here?"

"I don't know, maybe five years. I was a different person last time I was here. They kicked me out. I was kinda wild, I guess."

"You haven't been in touch since then?"

"Not really," he mumbled quietly. "I was an asshole back then. Wouldn't listen to what anybody told me. Drank too much. Town wasn't big enough for me, I guess. Anyway, I was kinda hoping, you know, things would be better now. Guess that ain't happening."

"You thought you were going to stay here?"

"Sorta. Didn't really think about it."

"Got any relatives in town?"

"A coupla cousins. Maybe. Not sure they'd wanna see me."

"Don't be so hard on yourself," Phillips said encouragingly. "Tell you what, let's get a hotel for the night. I'll pay. You can look around tomorrow. Maybe you'll find someone."

"What about your interview?"

"My appointment's at eleven."

48

Adams said little while Phillips settled on a budget motel on State Road 27 on the outskirts of town. He was clearly agitated, stepping out of the room for a smoke several times. It was during one of these smoke breaks that he'd received a self-destructing text with a phone number and the word *Call*. He knew immediately it came from one of the Sovereigns. Using a voice encryption app, he called the number.

"Hey, Glen, this is Wiley. Thanks for calling. How's it going?"

"Not so good. The house I grew up in burned down."

"Bummer, man. Hey, the reason I'm calling is we need to get your phone back."

"You do? Why?"

"All the encryption stuff. The generals are a little paranoid. You know how they are. They want to wipe the phone, make sure there's nothing incriminating on it. We shoulda done it when you left."

"Can I mail it to you?" Adams said.

"Well, they sent me up to here to get it. I'm in Eau

Claire. I checked the bus schedule and it looks like it stopped in Chippewa Falls."

"I'm in Hayward. Just checked into a hotel."

"Really? How far away is that?"

"I don't know, took us an hour and half I guess."

"Us?"

"A guy gave me a ride and he went out for pizza."

"What guy?"

"Somebody I met in Detroit. We rode the bus to Chippewa Falls and then he rented a car and brought me here. Real nice guy. A teacher."

"Is that right? Well, I'm looking forward to seeing you. Which hotel you at? Is this teacher staying with you?"

"Yeah. He paid for the room. We got two queen beds. It's a place off highway 27. It's kinda in the country."

"How about I come up in the morning? Take you and your friend out for breakfast."

"That'd be great. Hope I'm not causing any trouble."

"No trouble at all."

49

CRAWFORD SAT ON THE EDGE OF THE MATTRESS AS THE call ended.

"Fuck," he said, throwing the phone on the bed, watching it bounce, surprising Michael Gerlach, his roommate. They'd taken rooms in a motel in Eau Claire to spend the night and were preparing to go out for dinner. Crawford had checked the bus route. He'd expected to find Adams in Chippewa Falls, not a hundred miles farther north in Hayward, a tiny dot on a map surrounded by forest. Worse, he was sharing a room with a stranger.

"What up?"

"He's with someone."

"No shit."

"Yeah, no shit. Christ, this is not good."

"Who's he with?"

"A teacher, he said. He said they rode the bus from Detroit and the guy rented a car to drive him to Hayward. Does that make sense to you? I mean, who does that?"

"I don't know. Could happen, I guess."

"What're the odds? This stinks. Something ain't right."

Crawford paced the room distractedly while the sergeant started playing a first-person shooter on his phone, his shoulders weaving left and right as the game progressed, sounds of gunfire and explosions erupting from its tinny speaker.

"Would you stop that?" Crawford said, irritated. "We need to think this through."

Gerlach pocketed the phone and waited for instructions as the major stopped pacing and lowered himself into an armless chair at a faux mahogany desk, where he settled into a thoughtful pose, his elbow on the desk, his hand propping his stubbled chin. Moments passed. Gerlach stifled an urge to continue playing his game.

"Get Tony and Benny in here. We need to get a move on."

50

Agent Phillips didn't think there was much risk in leaving Adams in the room while he went for the pizza, stopping for a six pack on the return trip to the motel. Relaxed but tired he looked forward to a well deserved night's sleep. As far as he was concerned, nobody knew they were there and it would give him a chance to make a status report. The assignment to make contact with Adams had happened so unexpectedly that he'd brought his credentials and Glock 23, which he stashed in his daypack after arriving at the Detroit bus station. He'd had only minutes to prepare and he hadn't expected it to last more than a day, two at the most. All he was supposed to do was act friendly and gather whatever intelligence he could during the ride. He had not planned to improvise, but that changed almost from the start.

Drowsy after devouring half the pizza and one of the beers, Phillips began to nod off. There was just enough space in the room to squeeze in the two beds, separated by a small end table with a mid-century table lamp. Phillips turned off the harsh ceiling light as soon as he had turned it on. A Proscan flatscreen TV rested on a small dresser facing the beds. Adams was surfing the channels. Phillips had gotten little rest since leaving Detroit and felt comfortable with his roommate who seemed trustworthy and honest. He thought that it would be safe to get some shuteye. Maybe he should have bought an energy drink instead of the beer, but it didn't occur to him at the time. Besides, his body wasn't giving him a choice. So he lay on top of the covers, pulled out the two pillows and, staring at the ceiling, closed his eyes while Adams settled on a rerun of Law & Order.

Adams heard a car pull into the parking lot not long after Phillips started snoring, its headlights doused so as not to light up the rooms. Propped against the headboard, cushioned by pillows, the TV sound barely audible, he glanced at his phone. It was nearly nine-thirty. Still dressed with his shoes on, he slipped off the bed and quietly cracked the door.

"What the fuck?" he muttered as two men exited the black Tahoe with the Michigan plates.The sky was dark, clear and studded with sparkling stars.

"Over here, guys," Adams whispered, as they stepped onto the concrete walkway that fronted the rooms, holding out the phone, as if that was all that Wiley Crawford wanted. "I wasn't expecting you till the morning."

It hadn't occurred to him that the Sovereigns wanted something more until Michael Gerlach, the driver, acting on a nod from the major, grabbed the phone roughly, put it in a pocket and forcibly pushed Adams backwards into the room until he fell lengthwise on his bed.

"Hey, what's going on?" Adams protested loudly.

"Shut up," the brawny Gerlach said sharply, expertly binding Adams's hands behind his back with a zip tie.

"What the fuck are you doing?"

"Shut up, motherfucker," Gerlach said, finishing the job with a strip of duct tape across Adams's mouth.

Crawford meanwhile switched on the ceiling light and rummaged through Phillips's daypack, which he'd found on the floor between the beds.

"Teacher my ass," he said, as the agent opened his eyes, blinded momentarily by the light.

"Who are you? What are you doing here?" Phillips demanded, as he tried to lift himself off the bed only to be thwarted by Gerlach's heavy hand.

"Special Agent Craig Phillips, I presume," Crawford said, examining the agent's credentials.

Energized by a rush of adrenaline, Phillips calculated the odds of winning a fight against the two men.

"No hero stuff," Crawford said. "Put your hands behind your back."

Phillips hesitated.

"Now," Crawford barked.

Gerlach pushed the agent's face down on the bed, zip-tied Phillips's hands behind his back and, having forced him into a sitting position against the headboard, bound his ankles. No sooner had this been done than the headlights from the second SUV swept across the curtained windows. Benny and Tony were still yammering about the Lions' chances of winning their division, a subject they'd exhausted multiple times on the drive, as they squeezed into the crowded room.

"I'm hungry," Benny said as he eyed the dorm fridge next to the dresser, pulling out the remainder of the six pack.

Gerlach grabbed it by one of the empty rings and handed it to Crawford.

"What's with that?" Tony complained.

"No time for that," Crawford said, shaking his head and setting the beer under his chair.

The plan had been to confiscate Adams's cell phone and bury his body in the woods. The FBI agent had complicated matters beyond recognition.

Crawford could feel the tension building. Unhappy about the beer, Tony and Benny started taunting the captives, poking at them, making sinister jokes. Using mapping apps on their phones, Crawford and Gerlach plotted a course that would take them into the middle of nowhere on State Highway 70.

"It's just a lot of trees, only a coupla tiny burgs," Gerlach said. "Should be plenty of places we could pull off and finish the job."

51

Around midnight, Benny drove Phillips's rental to an unpaved road off State Highway 27, ditching it in the woods. He wore gloves so as not to leave fingerprints. The SUVs followed, with the FBI agent in the back seat of the lead car. Though he was bound, his mouth wasn't taped. Phillips did his best to convince them to surrender, which resulted in laughter.

"I gotta hand it to you," Crawford said, riding shotgun, looking into the back seat. "You FBI guys don't give up, do you? For your information, we ain't surrendering to no illegitimate agency of an illegitimate government. Besides, seems to me you're the one who surrendered."

"You'll never get away with killing me," Phillips said. "No matter how long it takes, they'll find you and you'll get the death penalty for killing a federal agent."

"Right," Crawford said. "And how many prisoners actually get executed? It's been like what, over a decade? You don't scare me. Anyway, they ain't gonna find you and your buddy."

Warming to his subject, Crawford pressed Phillips about what Adams had told him about the Sovereigns.

"All he talked about was his religion and how he wanted to start a ministry in his hometown. We never got into a conversation about your organization."

"Yeah, sure."

"What's the point of talking if you're not going to believe me?"

"You're right. It's a waste of time," Crawford said, discontinuing the conversation as a pickup approached from the opposite direction.

"Maybe I do believe you," Crawford said as the truck passed. "Maybe the kid didn't say anything. He wasn't high up in the organization. There's a lot he doesn't know. I know you cops think the small fry will lead you to the big fish, but I don't think that's gonna happen here. But maybe you can help yourself."

"How's that?"

"Maybe you can tell us what you do know. I wasn't expecting to run into no big time FBI agent but maybe we turn the tables. We interrogate you instead of you interrogating Glen."

"I wasn't interrogating him."

"Whatever."

Crawford was watching the road and thinking about how he could squeeze information out of his captive when they passed tiny Loretta. As much as it jeopardized his mission, he also saw it as an opportunity to gain insight into what the Sovereigns saw as the government's assault on their civil and legal rights. Since Phillips had been stationed in Detroit, Crawford assumed the agent was familiar with his organization. Perhaps he was helping to build a case against them. But he couldn't properly interrogate him in the car. Things could get out of hand.

"So, how far you wanna go?" Gerlach asked. "Shouldn't we turn off somewhere soon and get it over with?"

The sign was attached to a tree. Crawford saw it as it flashed by as they passed County Road M. CABINS FOR RENT. That gave him an idea.

"Turn around," he said.

52

Jacob didn't know what to do. Eric Larsen thought they should try to escape. Craig Phillips, who had found a position on the bed that minimized his pain and somewhat alleviated his labored breath, encouraged his two companions to flee.

"I'm the one they want," he insisted, his voice raspy like an old man. "I'm no good to you. I'll just slow you down."

Having struggled to bring the agent to his cabin, Jacob couldn't disagree. The man was in bad shape. He probably had a cracked rib or two. He might have a punctured lung. Stationary on the bed, upright with his legs stretched out in front of him, he seemed to have a handle on his pain. But it was a precarious hold. Even a slight movement produced a grimace, as if he'd been stuck with a needle. It was only after Jacob described what he had seen and what had happened to Phillips that Larsen realized the extent of the problem.

"There's bound to be police coming," Larsen said hopefully. "All they gotta do is take the road I plowed. They can get up here in no time."

"If they see it. From what you said, where they killed the cop was at least a mile down the road," Jacob said.

"Besides, it's getting dark," the agent said hoarsely.

"Couldn't they use a chopper?"

"The county doesn't own one," Larsen said.

"Well, the state police then. They'd be involved, wouldn't they?"

"They don't fly when it's snowing like this. Especially not at night."

"This is getting us nowhere," Phillips said, leaning forward slightly as he spoke. "You know, I could use another one of those pills."

"You sure?" Jacob asked.

Phillips started coughing. Tears welled in his brown eyes. Jacob gave him a pill and a glass of water. The agent shook his head.

"I don't need the water," the agent said. "I just need to find the right position."

Jacob and Larsen exchanged glances. They started to move away from the bed to speak privately.

"Whatever you got to say, you can say it in front of me. I already told you to go for help."

"Well, we're not leaving you alone," Jacob said, looking at Larsen for confirmation. Larsen nodded in agreement.

"In that case, what's the plan?" Phillips asked.

53

"You know what kinda fuck up this is? It's the worst place you've ever been in your life," the major said as he, Gerlach and Tony huddled in the cramped, cold cabin.

"And maybe the last place," Gerlach said.

"Yeah, that too."

A gust of wind rattled the drafty windows. Snow fell heavily from a thick layer of clouds, reducing visibility to several hundred feet. The harsh light of an LED lantern clawed at the walls, making the cabin feel smaller than it was. After dragging Adams's frozen body into a corner, Crawford sent Gerlach out to fetch firewood.

"So, what are we gonna do?" Tony asked.

"I don't know," the major said quietly. "This whole operation has gone to shit."

"Are we gonna get outta here?"

"Sure, just walk out the door, for all the good it'll do you."

"I've never been on one of these things before."

Crawford sat at the table, his parka unzipped, his mind reviewing all the things that had gone wrong, from spending the night in town, the pointless killing of the deputy, the escape of an FBI agent whom they could've used as a hostage, and now being stranded in a cabin in a snowstorm. The blame laid at the feet of the generals who had changed their minds about letting Adams leave. If it weren't for them, he wouldn't be in this position. As far as he was concerned, he'd done his job properly. It was everyone else who screwed up.

"Why did you kill that fucking cop?" he asked, his voice rising.

Tony bowed his head sheepishly.

"Nobody told you to do it, right?"

"I don't know. I got out of the car and I saw the cop and, I don't know, I just thought that's what I was supposed to do. I thought it was a good idea at the time."

"You're a fucking private. You aren't supposed to have ideas."

Tony moved to the window overlooking the pond and peeked through the blinds. Snow had infiltrated the interior sill.

"Boy, it's really coming down now."

54

It didn't take long for Michael Gerlach to scavenge an armful of firewood from the adjacent cabin and start a fire in the cabin's pot-bellied stove. As heat returned to the room, the three stripped off their coats, warmed their hands over the stove and continued to assess their situation.

"I vote we get the hell outta here right now," the sergeant said emphatically.

"What about Benny?" Tony asked.

"What about Benny?"

"Don't we need him?"

"For all we know he's dead. Besides, if it weren't for him the FBI guy would be dead," Crawford said, his eyes on Tony.

"What about the FBI agent? He can identify us. We're fucked if he's alive."

"We don't know that he is," Gerlach said.

"He's gotta be in that cabin over there," Crawford said. "Shit. I wanna get outta here, too. But ...."

"We can't leave him behind, can we?" Gerlach asked rhetorically.

The more he thought about it, the angrier Crawford became. The two lowest ranking members of his crew had fucked up in a big way and now here he was trying to figure out how to clean up the mess. Served Benny right if he was dead. In fact, they'd be better off if he was dead. The same with Tony. He didn't trust either of them anymore. They'd proven themselves undisciplined, undeserving of their status as Sovereign soldiers. What he wanted to do more than anything else, other than waking up from the nightmare and discovering that it hadn't happened, was talk to Gerlach in private.

"I'm getting hungry," Crawford said. "Tony, there's a box of food in my trunk. Go get it, wouldya?"

Tony nodded. No question he was the low man on the totem pole. And the major had made it clear he'd fucked up big time. Maybe this was a way of getting back into his good graces. Hastily putting his parka on, he slung his AR-15 over his shoulder and approached the door.

"Why the fuck you takin' the gun?"

"They might be out there."

"Bullshit. Leave the gun," Crawford barked. "Go get the food. Now."

The young man mumbled under his breath, set the gun near the door, pushed the door more forcefully than needed and shut it harder than needed.

"What the fuck is up with him?" Gerlach asked.

55

"WE GOTTA COME UP WITH A PLAN TO SAVE ourselves," Crawford said gravely.

"No shit," the sergeant said.

"You and me."

"What about ...?"

"Fuck him. As far as I'm concerned he and that fool Benny got us into this mess. You got a problem with that?"

Gerlach shrugged.

"So, what's the plan?"

"We use the RPG on that cabin and then we send up Tony to clean up. If we're lucky, whoever's in the cabin gets blown away and we put a few rounds into our boy and we haul ass the way we came."

"You don't think the police won't have the road staked out?"

Crawford sighed. He knew his plan wasn't so much a plan as a chain of thought, emphasizing the chain, not the thought. There wasn't enough time to think things through.

"The police'll have snowmobiles, man," the sergeant said.

"Yeah, but they're not gonna come at night."

"And what about helicopters?"

"One thing I know about helicopters is they don't like to fly in snowstorms, so the weather is on our side for now."

Gerlach watched Crawford as he started pacing, squinting through the blinds, seeing nothing but a shroud of falling snow. Being from rural Michigan, he was accustomed to winter weather, didn't think of it as an impediment.

"Maybe we hoof it out," he said at length. "Go out in the opposite direction we came. With all this snow, maybe they won't see our tracks. Sure as hell they won't see them in the dark."

"Yeah, but it's dark. We'll have the same trouble they have."

"They won't be on foot. They'll be pissed off. Things never work the way you think when you're pissed off. At least they don't for me."

"Well, I'm pissed off."

"I know. That ain't gonna help. I don't mind it being just the two of us, but I don't want to take the car," the sergeant said. "Just sayin'."

56

Tony stomped through the snow, infuriated. The major had dissed him in front of the sergeant, had made him feel small, as if he'd done something wrong when all he tried to do was demonstrate how ready he was to go to war. The Sovereigns hated cops almost as much as they hated Jews and minorities, or so they claimed, which was one reason he joined. He wanted action, wanted to take a stand, and he was young enough that dying was little more than an abstraction, something that happened to other guys, like Glen.

But that's the way it was in an army. He was a private and Crawford was a major. The have nots and the haves. It was always that way. Some of the other guys had told him what it took to move up in the organization. You could be good at some skill that they needed or you could be a real bad ass, and since he had no marketable skills he showed what he was by killing a cop. He thought they'd give him a medal or at least an attaboy. Maybe he had the Sovereigns figured all wrong.

"I mean," he said to himself as he approached the cars,

"they fucking kidnap an FBI agent but I'm the one who screwed up. That's whack."

Focused on his anger, following the lead of his flash-light, Tony didn't see Benny hunched down behind the lead SUV until he nearly stumbled over him.

"What the fuck?" Tony blurted loudly.

"It's me, bro," Benny said, standing quickly.

"Jesus. You scared the shit outta me. I thought you was dead," Tony said, pointing his headlamp, which he held in his hand, at Benny's face.

Benny knocked the light out of Tony's hand.

"Why'd you do that?" Tony asked, reaching into the snow for the light.

"They might be watching."

"Who?"

Benny nodded in the direction of Jacob's cabin.

"I been watchin', waitin' to see if they were going to take a shot. What're you doing out here?"

"Ah, fucking Crawford sent me for food."

"You get into an argument?"

"I'll tell you about it later. It's fucked, as usual."

"Look who I found," Tony announced as he entered the cabin carrying a cardboard box filled with bags of chips and cookies.

"Hey, Benny," Gerlach said, amazed and confounded at the same time. "You're alive."

"Yep, alive and—"

"You're bleeding," Tony said, after Benny pulled back his hood.

"Am I?" Benny said, feeling his forehead. "So that's what it is. I thought it was sweat. Couldn't tell in the dark."

"It's drying up."

"Yeah. I guess I knocked my head or something. Anyway, I was out like a light for a while there."

Crawford approached Benny, briefly examined his wound.

"You'll be okay."

"So, what's the plan?" Benny asked.

"How's he doing?" Jacob asked when he returned to the cabin after surveilling the pond.

"I think the pills knocked him out," Larsen said quietly.

They'd given up on the idea of keeping a watch outside. The falling snow was wet and heavy and froze to their clothing.

"They got a light on," Jacob said, hanging his wet parka from a hook near the back door. "Far as I can tell, they're inside. Didn't see anyone down below. 'Course, visibility sucks but I think I woulda seen something."

"I tried to go online but couldn't get a signal," Larsen said. "I used your computer. Hope you don't mind."

"I don't have internet," Jacob said matter-of-factly, after glancing at the snoozing Phillips. "You know, I don't like the idea of leaving you two alone. Besides, I'm dog tired. I've already been down there once and back."

"I thought we decided."

"I know."

"You know the area," Larsen said. "I've never been here.

And he's not going anywhere. It's you or nobody. I'll have the rifle and you'll be back with the cavalry in no time."

Jacob wanted to believe Larsen but he knew retracing his steps through new snow to County Road M wasn't like hiking a trail. The sooner he started the better, but traveling at night in the woods was risky. One wrong step and he could find himself with a broken ankle or at the bottom of a ledge. How much help would he be then? And then there was the fatigue, the aching muscles, the cloudiness in his brain, as if parts of it had fallen asleep.

"We'll do like we said," Jacob said, unconvinced. "I wish I could get some sleep but I'm so wired I can't stand it."

"Too bad you can't take a pill like him."

"I probably wouldn't wake up for days," Jacob said, rising from the table. "I think I'll have another cup."

59

TONY GOT OVER HIS ANGER AS SOON AS THE MAJOR outlined the plan. More than anything, he wanted to see the RPG slam into the cabin. He'd seen them on videos and TV but never in real life. But he'd be there to watch it turn the cabin into kindling and the part he liked most was that he and Benny would be the cleaners, finishing off any survivors. It showed that even though the major had criticized him openly, he still trusted him enough to take on an important assignment.

"Maybe I shouldn't have shot the cop," he told Benny after Crawford had spelled out his plan.

"Maybe not. Everybody was surprised."

"Especially the cop," Tony said mockingly.

Benny shook his head.

"You think it's funny to kill someone like that?"

"No, no. That's not what I meant. I was just trying to, you know, be funny now. I just thought at the time that, you know, I'd get more respect."

"Trouble is, Tony, you weren't thinking. You don't do

nothing on your own. We're an army, not a bunch of gang-bangers."

Tony hadn't seen Benny's serious side before. He'd always thought of him as a cut up, a class clown. But he wasn't clowning around.

"I know that," Tony said, defensively. "I learned a lot on this trip. A lot."

"Me too. I thought I was gonna die, you know," Benny said earnestly. "The truck bouncing all over the place and then the lights go out. And when I come to and I'm runnin' away trying to keep from falling on the ice I'm thinking every second that I was gonna get a bullet in the back, that I wouldn't make it."

"But you did make it."

Benny smiled as they exchanged fist bumps.

"You know, I'm gonna do everything I can to make things right with the major," Tony said solemnly.

60

With the forest shrouded in darkness, they made their way from the cabin up to the road where they'd left the cars, high-stepping their way through the deep snow. The tire tracks were filling in with new snow. The cars were parked so that their sides faced the pond, giving them plenty of cover.

"I don't think they can see us through the woods," Gerlach said, as he sized up his position. "It's almost a straight shot. I was afraid I'd be shooting uphill, but this is almost perfect."

Rocket propelled grenades were hard to come by. The RPG-7 launcher in the trunk of Crawford's car was the only one in the Sovereigns' arsenal.

Gerlach had fired it once during a training exercise and remembered how the fifteen-pound launcher rested easily on his shoulder. He had hoped to watch the rocket shoot out of the barrel and track it to its target, but smoke got into his eyes and he saw nothing. Although the ear protectors he wore blocked out most of the sound, his ears were ringing for an hour after he fired. It wasn't until he saw his companions giving each other high fives and jumping up and down that he realized he'd hit the target.

"We didn't bring the ear protectors?" he asked to no one in particular as he lifted the launcher out of the trunk.

"I guess not," Crawford said. "Benny, you were in charge of—"

"I just took what was there, major. Didn't see no ear plugs."

"They weren't ear plugs," Gerlach said testily. "They were like big fucking ear muffs."

"Well, I didn't see them. They weren't on the shelf," Benny protested. "I was told to get the RPG. Nobody said anything about ear muffs."

"Fucking great," the sergeant said. "I shoot this off, I'm gonna blow out my ear drums."

"Okay, okay," Crawford said. "Let's just figure this out."

"You can use my earbuds, if you want," Tony volunteered.

"Thanks, but no thanks."

"You got a better idea?"

Gerlach leaned the launcher against the car and rifled through the cargo space, pulling out a black long-sleeved thermal from a small duffel bag and a pair of wool socks. Tearing the arms off, he knotted them together and wrapped the material loosely around his head, making sure it covered his ears. Then he folded the socks and inserted one against each ear before tightening the material.

"I think this'll work," he said as he loosened the sleeves, removing the socks.

"Gimme your earbuds," he said, holding his hand toward Tony. Pressing the buds into his ears, he tightened the cloth around his head, installed the socks and directed Tony to tie the ends together

"Say something," Gerlach said.

"What you want me to say?" Tony responded.

The sergeant gave a thumbs up.

"This'll do."

Gerlach estimated the distance to the cabin at two hundred feet from where he stood, give or take. With the wind at his back, he felt confident that he could hit the cabin full on into its heavy timbers.

He figured the projectile needed to strike something hard to do the most damage. A perfect shot would enter through a window and explode against a back wall. Loading the rocket into the launcher himself, he moved away from the cars to a position where in daylight he would be totally exposed. Packing down the snow with his shoes, he tested the ground to make sure it wouldn't give way. He removed the rocket's safety pin and glanced back at Crawford, who stood behind the cars. Benny and Tony had stepped away from the cars to get a better view of the shot. Tony held his phone in front of his face to record it. Both jabbered quietly, excitedly. Crawford gave a thumbs up and the sergeant took aim.

61

Even though they had decided not to conduct regular watches, Jacob had reached the point where not even caffeine could keep him from nodding off. The skiing and snowshoeing, the enormous amount of energy it took to pull Phillips through the snow and up the hill to his cabin had left him feeling hollow and shaky, a shell of the robust woodsman that had started the day. Even his emotions were rebelling, putting him on edge to the point that he didn't know whether to cry or scream. But these were things he would never think of sharing, especially now. Larsen had had a bad day. Phillips had it worse. He knew he had to suck it up but his brain was telling him to take a nap.

"I'm gonna get some fresh air," he announced as he grabbed the binoculars and stepped outside, leaving his parka behind, thinking the cold air would act as a tonic against his fatigue.

"Where's the firewood?" Larsen asked. "It's starting to cool down in here."

"Good idea. There's a stack behind the house. It's just

up the hill a bit," Jacob said as the two men converged on the back door."

Making his way to the edge of his property where it merged with the forest, Jacob crouched in the brush, wishing he'd brought his coat. The snow was heavy and wet and it was coming down with no let up. He had a decent view of the cabins below, obscured somewhat by the falling snow but not hidden by the shadowy, encompassing woods. Through the binoculars he could see light-colored smoke drifting from the cabin's chimney. A light was on. Glassing the pond, he saw that the trail he'd left pulling the sled had almost filled in. Another hour of this, he thought, and it would be gone. Not that it mattered. They knew where he was. He also knew they weren't after him, that if he simply walked away he would be safe.

He couldn't see his cabin from his overlook. The brush was thick and he was nearly one hundred feet away. But his eye caught movement on the opposite side. Nothing he could identify. Nothing definite. Just movement of some kind. Just as he put his glass on the shadows he was momentarily blinded by a jet of flame erupting out of the darkness. The sound was unmistakable. He couldn't even turn his head before the projectile exploded, debris falling everywhere, the smell of smoke and burnt lumber filling the air. Instinctively, he flattened himself. At his distance, he felt the ground tremble followed by a concussive wave.

Seconds passed before he lifted his head. Then he looked at the other side. He could hear cheering. What could he do? He was unarmed, wet and cold. For all he knew, his companions were dead, and even if they weren't he wasn't an EMT. What could he do for them?

62

THE MAJOR AND GERLACH LOOKED AT EACH OTHER IN bafflement. Benny, who had been jumping up and down and pointing when the grenade launched, stopped abruptly when the cabin failed to explode.

"What the fuck?" the major said.

The aim was as good as could have been expected, the grenade crashing through the front window, but instead of turning the cabin into kindling it raised the roof several feet and blew open the front door. The building seemed to be intact.

"I don't know, Wiley," the sergeant said as he tore off his improvised ear protection. "Maybe it was a dud. Fuck."

Tony waited for the cabin to explode and when it didn't he stopped recording the event with his phone and shook his head.

"What the fuck?"

"Yeah, what the fuck?" Benny echoed.

"It's a fucking dud," Gerlach howled as he threw the launcher into the snow.

"Goddammit," Crawford sputtered. "After all the shit we've been through, now this."

Clearly, there was a problem with the grenade. Though they couldn't see the rear of the cabin, the front wall had bowed outward in places but remained intact. Parts of the roof had caved when it settled and streamers of smoke curled through the open doorway. Crawford, Tony and Benny gathered around Gerlach.

"It didn't feel right when it launched," he said.

Even so there was no doubt that the grenade had damaged the cabin.

"Think we got 'em?" Crawford asked.

"Looks like we did," Tony said.

"I wasn't asking you," Crawford said sharply.

Tony bristled. Benny put a sympathetic hand on the private's shoulder.

"Take it easy, bro," he whispered.

"I don't know," Gerlach said.

"Tony, go up there and check it out," Crawford said. "Finish them off. You're good at that."

Tony grabbed his AR, but Crawford stopped him.

"Use your nine mil, private. Ain't nobody up there gonna fight back."

Tony's anger melted as he handed his rifle to the major. Maybe Crawford wasn't dissing him so much as testing him. In either case, he felt relief as he descended to the pond. This was more like it. Blowing up things. Killing the enemy. his main disappointment being that the building didn't explode. At least he had a video to prove what they did. He couldn't wait to get back to Michigan and show the guys. But he had an important job to do first.

"Before you go, give me your phone," Crawford said.

"What? Why?"

"Just give it to me," the major said, holding his hand out.

"I was gonna video the cabin, you know."

"Just give me the fucking phone," Crawford insisted.

"Fuck," Tony mouthed, pulling it out of his pocket and pressing it into Crawford's hand.

The major could take the fun out of a carnival, he thought as he descended to the pond. How many times would he get the chance to make a video like that? He thought he would be doing the Sovereigns a favor. They could use the video as propaganda and for recruiting, like ISIS. But he reminded himself he was a soldier and a soldier had to follow orders, no matter what. So, he followed the beam of his headlamp, trotting across the snow-covered pond and up the snowy slope, emerging less than fifty feet from the smoldering structure. Poking his head inside the doorway he could see that the interior was in shambles with part of the back wall blown outward though it, too, was still functional. It was smoky inside but he couldn't see any flame. Everything seemed to be covered in black soot that was settling like snow. Pine boards were strewn across the floor like a game of pick up sticks played by giants. The clutter obscured everything. Even with the headlamp, it was difficult to make out objects, obscured by the impenetrable darkness and smoke.

"Where are the bodies?" he said as he rotated his head, squinting into the crevices and gaps under the lumber, his pistol in his right hand.

After several minutes of searching, some of the boards so jammed up that he couldn't budge them, he stepped outside, moved to the edge of the overhang and called out.

"I need help," he shouted. "There's too much—"

The muzzle flash was unmistakable. But he never knew what hit him as the round tore through his chest before his brain could register what his eyes saw. He was already gone as he collapsed in a heap in the snow, his last breath steaming from between his suddenly silent lips.

63

Benny couldn't believe what Gerlach had done.

"What the fuck? What the fucking fuck?" he shouted, jumping in place.

Crawford cut Benny off in seconds.

"Shut up," he barked. "We've got work to do. I want you to go down there and set our cabin on fire."

Stunned, Benny hesitated before responding, his momentary joy replaced by disbelief and confusion. How could they do this to one of their own? The narrative he'd invented as to how things would work out had been ripped from his hands. One minute he and Tony were celebrating and the next Tony was dead. It wasn't supposed to work out like that.

"What do I put it in?" Benny asked finally, his voice betraying his agitation.

"We got water bottles up the ass," Gerlach said.

"Mike, you go with him." the major ordered. "Make sure it gets done right."

Benny felt the hairs on the back of his neck stand up as he went through the motions of siphoning gas into a plastic bottle. Was he next? His mind raced in multiple directions. Bottle in hand, he grabbed Tony's AR as he started to make his way to the cabin.

"Leave the gun here," the sergeant said. "I'm not taking mine. We're done killing for now."

Benny liked the sergeant. He'd always treated him fairly, unlike Crawford who sometimes got into his face.

"So, you're not gonna kill me like Tony?" Benny asked.

"No way," Gerlach said reassuringly. "Tony wasn't working out."

"You'd tell me if I'm not working out, right?"

"It's like they say, if you ain't being yelled at it's because you ain't worth it."

Benny felt relieved. People were always yelling at him.

64

THE EXPLOSION FRIGHTENED HIM. WITH EVERY STEP Jacob tried to convince himself going for help was the right thing to do. He wouldn't be running away. He could help them with minor injuries, not those from an RPG. But the farther he went, the more he realized he wasn't dressed for it nor would he be able to maintain his pace. And then he heard a shot from across the pond.

Had they finished his friends off? How he wished he had a gun. Just goes to show mistakes happen. Fail to take an umbrella on a cloudy day, and it rains. Jacob was astonished at how quickly things normalized after he and Phillips had reached the cabin, as if the killers had taken a timeout on account of snow. What was he thinking? The old normal had been replaced by the new normal as easily as changing sheets on a bed. Not keeping watch turned out to be a bad idea. Now he had to make up for it. There seemed to be no choice, not in his present state of mind.

Sneaking around in the woods was easy for him. He knew how to take cover, he knew how to wait. He knew how to walk in silence. And he was patient, approaching the rear of the cabin, which, if the roof hadn't been raised to one side, looked sound. The side wall had a gap in it where there had been a window. The framing and siding around it had blown out, broken planks scattered across the snow. Nothing was moving on his side of the pond, though he could hear voices and other noises from the other side. He couldn't make out words, but he knew they weren't coming from Phillips or Larsen. The back door was jammed shut so he clambered through the window opening. He paused, sniffing the acrid air. He listened.

And then he heard something from behind the cabin. Careful not to trip over debris, he found Larsen splayed out across the firewood. It was so dark that he could make out few details. The big man lay face down across the wood pile where the explosive concussion had dropped him.

"You okay?" Jacob whispered.

Larsen moaned.

"My back," he groaned.

Jacob reached toward his injured companion as if to help him sit up.

"Don't," Larsen said. "I'm okay if I don't move. God, it hurts."

"You sure?"

"Yeah. How's Craig?"

"I'll check."

Nothing inside the cabin was where it should have been except the stove, which had remained erect, semi-connected to its exhaust pipe, the cast iron sides hot to the touch, smoke wafting through a gash in the pipe. The table had been crushed by a joist. Where had he left his rifle? Wasn't it on the table? Feeling his way blindly in the interior darkness he was careful not to make noise. If he could hear them, they could hear him, he reasoned. And turning his headlamp on was out of the question. But there was no way he could find anything without a light and he feared that feeling around, reaching into dark recesses might do more harm than good. He could inadvertently push his hand through an exposed nail or a splinter.

Progress was slow. Despite the cold, sweat beaded on his forehead. It seemed to him that he'd been at it for hours but only minutes had passed. His exhaustion was making him edgy, impatient. Finding the rifle had become the most important thing he'd ever done in his life. He was determined to succeed, even if the gun was in pieces. There was nothing else he could do. He was not going to let them get away with it. He was not going to go for help. He wanted to scream and then he heard car doors open and shut loudly on the other side. An engine started, the driver holding the accelerator down as if to hear the big eight-cylinder beast roar. The headlights came on as Jacob gingerly flattened himself against the debris.

They were getting away.

65

GERLACH AND BENNY HAD BEEN EFFICIENT IN splashing gasoline throughout the cabin. Standing outside the open back door, the sergeant watched as Benny used a butane lighter to ignite a pine sprig, which he threw into the emptiness, its flames spreading across the floor like tentacles. They could feel the heat as they backed away, carrying the LED lanterns. By the time they'd reached the cars, bright flames licked at the doorway.

"We need to get going," the major said sternly as Benny quickly climbed into the back seat while Gerlach got behind the wheel. Crawford nodded, Gerlach put the transmission in reverse and slowly backed out until they'd reached the first curve where there was enough room to get the car headed in the right direction.

"Kill the lights," Crawford said.

Gerlach stopped as soon as the lights went out.

"I can't see much," he said, despite the daytime driving lights being on.

"Go slow then. Nobody's following us."

Benny watched anxiously, sitting on the edge of the

seat, nervously running a thumb and forefinger back and forth across his lips. He had an even worse view of the road ahead.

"Careful, we don't wanna go over the edge," he said, nervously.

"Shut up," the sergeant growled, as he put the automatic into low gear, tapping the brakes on descents and accelerating slightly on inclines.

Crawford knew their only hope of escape depended on the snow not letting up and the fact that the logging road they were on exited a mile away from where Tony had killed the deputy. That and the darkness. Even though it slowed them down, he believed the responders wouldn't take the chance of driving into the woods at night. They may have been angry but they weren't desperate like he was.

"We're gonna make it, right, major?"

"That's the plan, Benny. That's the plan."

66

It wasn't until the car had made the first turn that Jacob stepped through the open front door onto the skirt of land fronting the cabin where he could see the body, lying face up in the snow, the glow of a headlamp nearby. Holding his headlamp in his hand, he realized immediately that the body didn't belong to Craig Phillips.

"What the fuck?" he said as he leaned over the young killer. "They killed their own guy?"

Returning to his task quickly, he turned on his headlamp, found a pair of gloves hanging from the back wall and used them to work his way through the rubble, until he'd cleared enough that he could see everything that had been thrown to the floor in the area of the table. The table top was lodged at an angle, having been stabbed by a board. Standing, he leaned forward, aiming his headlamp this way and that, stopping at what looked like the tip of his Winchester's barrel, which he pulled. It gave several inches and then caught on something. Pulling as hard as he could, he realized the nylon sling was holding it back. Sawing through the sling with his folding knife, he nearly fell over backwards as he gave the barrel a final tug.

It wasn't much to look at. The telescopic sight had been crushed but the magazine was in place. Pulling on the bolt, he loaded a round from the magazine and set the safety. He knew what he had to do. He wanted to chase after them. He was familiar with the territory, knew the short cuts. The only tool he had was his knife and he used it to remove the screws that attached the scope to the rifle. It had been fortunate that he had cut the strap near the center. There was enough slack that he could tie the ends together. Standing in front of the cabin, he hesitated. Was someone moaning, or was it the wind? He looked behind him into the darkness.

"Craig, is that you?"

Stepping inside, he saw a hand sticking out of the debris where the bed had been, his headlamp throwing a circle of light at his feet. Near the hand, a soot-blackened face revealed itself.

"Are you okay?"

"Go. Get 'em," the FBI agent said hoarsely. "Don't let them get away."

Jacob listened momentarily to the agent's labored breath.

"I shouldn't leave you."

"Go, you can't let them get away."

"What about you?"

"Never mind me. Don't argue. Just go. I'm stuck but I'm okay."

Jacob was bent on revenge and needed little encouragement. There was no time to waste if he was going to catch up to them.

Ignoring the falling snow and cold, his clothing damp

from sweat and snow, not finding his parka, he followed the beam of the headlamp down the hill, the nearby forest lit by the flaming cabin at the far end of the pond.

67

GERLACH STRUGGLED TO KEEP THE CAR FROM VEERING off the road. Between the protruding rocks and ruts, the front wheels had a mind of their own, even at a crawl.

"Can you go a little faster?" Crawford urged. "We'll never get there at this rate."

"You want me to run off the road?" the driver grumbled, his eyes glued to the windshield. "I can't see the road."

"Hey, guys," a voice in the back seat cautioned. "Let's not argue."

"Fuck you, Benny," Gerlach snarled. "It's your fault we're in this mess."

"Hey, I'm not the one in charge."

Crawford shook his head. It wasn't Benny's fault. It was the generals' fault for changing their minds. They're the ones who sent Adams on his way. No matter how much he thought about it he would never be able to understand it. But he had bigger, more immediate problems. If it came to it, if they reached the road and it was swarming with police, what would he do? Was it worth dying as a consequence of his leaders' bad decision? It was one thing to sacrifice himself for a cause, but he couldn't help but think he would be dying to erase someone else's mistake. Where was the glory in that?

68

Jacob wasn't sure what he would do when he caught up with them, though he had no doubt that he would. There wasn't enough light in the dark forest to see clearly and he turned off his headlamp to avoid being seen. Everything was shrouded in shadows. The first time he saw the car, it was inching down a slope toward a sharp bend. He brought his rifle to his shoulder and sighted. He couldn't see anything through the dark, tinted windows. The best he could do would be to put a bullet through the front passenger window and hope that it hit someone. The only way to get a clear shot would be to fire through the windshield. To do it he'd have to be standing on the road. But what if he missed? He'd be exposed. They'd see him. To his mind the best shot, the safest shot, was through the side window. However, by the time he'd made up his mind, his opportunity had passed.

The adrenaline rush he'd felt when he started the chase had played out quickly. He had ignored his fatigue as he ran up and down rugged hills, the rifle banging against his back with every step. But his strength had diminished and he became aware of it as soon as he stopped to take aim a second time. He struggled to hold the weapon steady. The tip of the barrel seemed to have a mind of its own. But locating the vehicle was simple as the driver was riding his brakes. He could still get a shot but he'd need something to steady the gun. They may as well have had their headlights on, he thought. But he was glad they didn't. He might not have been able to keep up if they did.

Even so, with each passing minute they were getting closer to County Road M and escape. If he was going to stop them, he was going to have to do it before they topped the final rise, after which it was all downhill. But when he got there he couldn't catch his breath. Bent over, his hands on his knees, steam gushing out of his mouth, he felt weak, light headed, his chest heaving. They were almost there now as he struggled to tame his breath. But he couldn't hold the rifle steady. The barrel wobbled. Straightening, looking around frantically, he moved to a stunted Norway pine. At shoulder height was a thin branch covered in needles. But it flexed as he nestled the forestock across it, causing the weapon to slide off. Pressing the gun in the crook where the branch joined the trunk, aiming just as the car reached the top of the hill, he exhaled.

69

Michael Gerlach could see the brake lights in the rear view. He knew they were lighting up the forest like Christmas. But he didn't say anything. What were they going to do, cover them with duct tape? He couldn't afford to think about it, not now that he was beginning to believe they would make it. Not a word from him. Nothing to jinx it. They were at a place where the road rose sharply toward a crest beyond which he couldn't see. But going uphill, he didn't have to ride the brakes. It wasn't until they reached the top that he lost sight of the narrow road. Gripped by fear, he slammed on the brakes and turned the headlights on.

"What the fuck are you doing?" Crawford shouted just as blood sprayed from Gerlach's head.

The .308 round coming through the passenger window had found its mark, slamming the driver's head against the side window. For a moment it seemed that time had stopped. Michael had yet to turn the wheel but his foot was no longer on the brake pedal and the car lurched forward, the wheels aimed at the steep slope instead of following the road to the right.

Crawford grabbed at the steering wheel, his face dripping with his sergeant's gore. But gravity had its way, sending the SUV down the slope, slowly at first and then like an out-of-control roller coaster, the right side smashing into a stump that turned the car sideways, which was all it took to start it tumbling obliquely once, twice, thrice before wrapping itself around a tree, coming to a rest on its crushed roof, most of its windows obliterated, Crawford's door flung open like the top of a soup can.

Benny lay awkwardly in the back across the roof, his legs pinned to the seat, his skinny neck twisted grotesquely. Crawford couldn't focus his eyes as he lay on his back. He couldn't see or feel the fibula protruding from his left leg or the gash in his forehead where he'd hit the dashboard. He saw a light and closed his eyes. It looked red through his eyelids. Then the air started to fill with the sound of bees. How strange, he thought. Where would bees come from? Where were they? Why were they here? And then he heard something else. Words.

"Over here," Jacob shouted. "Over here," he waved, pointing his rifle at the injured man's head.

And as the bees came closer they turned into snowmobiles.

THE END

ABOUT THE AUTHOR

John Koloen, a native of Wisconsin, has been a longshore-man, construction worker, newspaperman, magazine publisher and bureaucrat. He lives in Galveston, TX, with his wife Laura. He is the author of five novels.

To receive updates on John's upcoming books, please signup for the free newsletter at watchfirepress.com/jk.

69331871R00112

Made in the USA
San Bernardino, CA
14 February 2018